The Princess School

If the Shoe Fits

The Princess School

If the Shoe Fits

Jane B. Mason ❧ Sarah Hines Stephens

SCHOLASTIC INC.

New York Toronto London Auckland Sydney
Mexico City New Delhi Hong Kong Buenos Aires

Copyright © 2004 by Jane B. Mason and Sarah Hines Stephens

All rights reserved.
Published by Scholastic Inc.
SCHOLASTIC and associated logos are trademarks and/or registered trademarks of Scholastic Inc.

ISBN 0-439-54532-3

12   11   10   9   8   7   6   4 5 6 7 8 9/0

Printed in the U.S.A.   40

First printing, February 2004

For David and Anica, with thanks for the royal treatment.

—JBM & SHS

Chapter One
Ella

"Ouch!" Ten-year-old Ella Brown's bare foot came down on a sharp rock. Lifting the skirts of her hand-me-down gown, she hopped on her left foot to inspect her right. No damage, just dirt.

I should be used to dirt, she thought grimly.

With a sigh, she continued gingerly down the lane, picking the least muddy path. She wished yet again that she had a decent pair of shoes for her first day of Princess School.

Her old shoes were full of holes and blackened with soot — too shabby to wear, even with a secondhand dress. They were fine for chores, but not for Princess School. At Princess School the right pair of shoes could make all the difference. Ella ought to know.

Biting her lip, Ella remembered the mysterious shoes that had arrived the night before her Princess School entrance interview — the grueling interrogation every prospective princess faced in order to gain admittance. The shoes sparkled in their velvet-lined box. A small bow shimmered on each curved toe. They were perfect! Until she put them on. As soon as they were on her feet, Ella realized they were much too big.

Of course she had worn them to the interview anyway. Even though they were made of glass, too big, and *really* uncomfortable, they were better than the grubby slippers she had. Ella would rather go barefoot than be seen entering Princess School in *those*.

She stepped over a small puddle in her path and sighed again. It was, quite simply, a miracle that she had been accepted at Princess School at all. And Ella was pretty sure she knew who to thank for it. The telltale sparkle on those new shoes, and the fact that her fairy godmother had recently accepted a job in the Princess School administrative chambers, could only mean one thing. Somebody had been up to a little bobbity-boo.

Ella smiled. Her fairy godmother, Lurlina, looked out for Ella when no one else did. She didn't always get things exactly right . . . like the time she was trying to help clean and decided to banish all of the dust and pet hair from the house. The poor cat was bald for months. But Lurlina *almost* always made things better. And this morning Ella was counting on that.

She hoped Lurlina could make her some new shoes with a quick wave of her wand (and get the size right this time). All Ella had to do was get to Princess School early enough to find her fairy godmother without anyone noticing she was barefoot. That shouldn't be too hard, right?

Looking down, Ella saw her muddy toes peeking out from under her dress. If she bent her knees slightly and walked with her back straight, her hem brushed the ground (gathering *more* dirt), but it hid her feet completely.

"This just might work," Ella said to herself, half smiling.

Then she rounded the corner and the gleaming towers of Princess School came into view. They pierced the sky like jeweled points on a crown. Beneath the stone spires, the enormous arched entrance was swarming with gilded carriages, teams of horses, coachmen, servants, and dozens of novice princesses.

Ella's bent knees suddenly felt weak.

For the first time in her life, Ella wished she were sitting in the kitchen peeling potatoes or sweeping cinders back into the fireplace. At least there she knew what she was doing. It was awful to admit, but she felt more at home in front of the hearth than in a school full of girls in gowns.

How will I ever fit in here? Ella wondered. Doubt swept over her as she realized she wasn't at all sure she would. As she gazed at the fanciful scene before her, she felt the urge to turn and run.

' Suddenly the pounding of hooves and rattling of wheels jolted her out of her thoughts. Just in time she dove out of the way of a speeding coach. By pressing against the bushes on the side of the road she only barely managed to keep from being run down.

The coach whizzed past in a blur of blue and gold. One of the large, spoked wheels bumped into a rut in the road and a shower of mud splashed onto Ella's skirts.

With her heart beating fast and her fists clenched in anger, Ella peered after the racing carriage. It was her father's coach! And the piercing cackles and disgusting, snorting laughs echoing out of the windows were all too familiar. Her lying stepsisters!

What were Hagatha and Prunilla doing in her father's coach? Ella fumed. That morning, after Ella served them breakfast, Hag and Prune told their mother they were getting a ride to Princess School with Prince Hargood.

"Such a waste to send the whole coach for just one girl," Ella's stepmother, Kastrid, had said. She flashed a crooked smile as Ella cleared the breakfast dishes and hurried downstairs to finish pressing Hagatha's gown and Prunilla's hair ribbons. "Ella, you can walk."

Ella knew Hag and Prune had lied on purpose. She swiped at her skirts angrily. They couldn't get over the fact that Ella was starting at *their* school — and heaven forbid they should all arrive together! The older girls didn't think Ella could make it at Princess School.

Ella had hoped that starting Princess School would change things at home. That her stepsisters would stop ordering her around and insulting her. That her stepmother would stop treating her like hired help. That her father would stand up to his new wife. But if today's start was any indication, nothing had changed, and nothing ever would.

"There's no way I'm going to spend the rest of my life in my stepmother's kitchen," Ella said out loud, giving her skirts a final swipe. She would show her awful stepsisters she was as good as they were, even with a muddy dress and bare feet.

Bent knees wobbling, Ella headed for the drawbridge that led up to the school's entrance. Several long-necked white swans glided in the moat beneath the bridge.

They look more regal than I do, Ella thought. She held her head a little higher. If she was going to get in unnoticed, she had to look like she belonged. Luckily most of the other students were too excited to pay attention to a shabbily dressed new girl. But Ella found it difficult not to stare at them. They were lovely, with fancily braided and coiled hair. They wore gowns of every color — in silk and velvet and brocade. The fine fabrics glimmered in the sun. Clustered in small groups, the girls chatted animatedly with one another, making polite princess gestures with delicate fingers.

Ella looked past them toward the school entrance and her heart jumped. The white marble steps up to the school were so polished, the sun glinted off them. The carved wooden doors were as ornate as any gilded picture frame, and when a princess or member of the faculty stepped up to them, the heavy doors opened with a quiet *whoosh*. It sounded as if the castle itself were drawing a breath.

On either side of the doors, trumpeters raised long golden instruments to their lips. Then, with a few short blasts, they announced that the first day of the new school year was about to begin.

As she gazed at the castle that was to be her new school, Ella was filled with awe . . . and dread. Her stepsisters were right: She would never make it at Princess School.

You can't think like that, she scolded herself. *Be confident. You can do this.*

Ella squinched up her toes and walked more quickly

toward the steps. She needed to find Lurlina before class started. But with each step, she passed another perfect princess-in-training and her courage began to melt away. It seemed every novice she walked by was more beautiful than the last. They were all so well pressed and dressed!

Here I am in dirty rags, and I don't even have shoes on! Ella thought. *Lurlina* has *to come through.*

At the base of the stairs, Ella stopped in her tracks when she saw the prettiest girl yet. Her hair was the color of wheat in the sun. Her cheeks were like rose blossoms. Her eyes were bluer than the clearest lake.

"Do be careful, dear," the girl's mother cooed while her father wrung his hands nearby.

"Won't you please wear these gloves?" her father begged, holding out a pair of metal gauntlets suitable for a knight.

The beautiful girl smiled kindly at her parents, refusing the hand armor. Tiny fairies buzzed all around her, adjusting her collar, twisting an already-perfect curl, smoothing her delicate eyebrows, draping her skirts more elegantly down the stairs, twittering their advice in her ears.

Ella almost laughed out loud at the bustling fairies. What could they possibly do to make this girl more lovely?

Forgetting all about her own predicament, Ella

lifted her skirts to climb the stairs, the final ascent into Princess School. With a gasp, she saw her own pale naked foot shining like the moon on the stone stair. She quickly dropped her skirts back over it and looked around to see if anyone else had noticed. No one turned in her direction, except the beautiful girl with the fairies.

Ella stared into the other girl's deep blue eyes and waited. She waited for her to say something mean. To laugh and point. She waited to be ridiculed. Exposed as a fake. Thrown out of school! But all she saw in the other girl's eyes was curiosity.

"What is it, Rose?" the girl's mother asked anxiously.

"Are you afraid? Do you want me to come with you?" Rose's father asked, looking around to see what had caught his daughter's eye. "I can call the guards."

"Please, Father, it's nothing." Rose brushed her parents off with a smile. "I'm fine. And I'm going to school now. *Alone.*"

Ella watched, shocked and grateful, as the girl strode confidently up the stairs without so much as another glance in her direction. All eyes, it seemed, were on Rose. Ella took a cautious look around to see if anyone else had seen her. She could still make it inside unnoticed. Except . . .

Leaning against a banner pole, another girl peered

at her with an odd smile. The girl had an unbelievably huge coil of auburn hair piled haphazardly on her head, and her navy dress was strange — shorter than Ella's and looser. But before Ella could decipher the look on her face, the girl turned away and waved, not very royally, to a prince on the other side of the rose garden.

The prince returned the wave with a grin and then ducked inside an enormous manor house. Ella squinted into the distance. The sign over the door read THE CHARM SCHOOL FOR BOYS.

Ella's stomach gave a lurch. The Charm School! Every prince in the kingdom went there! And princes made her almost as nervous as princesses. Ella sighed. Why did *everything* make her so nervous?

With her feet hidden, knees bent, and stomach fluttering, Ella walked up the last few stairs and stepped through the already-open doors of her new school.

She felt her breath catch in her throat. The inside of Princess School was as overwhelming as the outside. The polished stone floor was an ornate pattern of square pink and white stones. The tall, narrow, diamond-paned windows reached from the floor to the ceiling, ending in delicately pointed tops. The ceiling itself was silver leaf, while the alabaster pillars between the endless arches were covered with carved roses and ivy.

Excited voices echoed loudly off the tall arches. Teachers stood in the glittering foyer, directing new students to class. For a moment Ella couldn't even move. Prospective princesses swarmed past her. Which way was her fairy godmother's chamber?

A woman in a red velvet gown approached Ella. "Your name?" she asked, eyeing Ella's mud-strewn gown warily.

"Cinderella Brown," Ella replied, her heart sinking. Out of the corner of her eye she could see the girl who'd been waving excitedly to the Charm School boy outside. She seemed to be watching Ella with renewed interest. A trumpet blast echoed down the hall, interrupting Ella's thoughts and distracting the other girl. There would not be enough time to find Lurlina before class. Ella would have to start Princess School barefoot and filthy.

Chapter Two

Rapunzel

Rapunzel followed the barefoot girl with the filthy gown into the large hearthroom and sat down in a velvet-cushioned, high-backed chair. The hearthroom was big and echoey, like most of the rooms in a castle. A fire burned in the grate of a large fireplace to take away the morning chill. Tapestries depicting kings and queens doing things kings and queens do lined the walls. But Rapunzel wasn't really looking at the furnishings. She was looking at the other girls. And she was scowling.

Okay, maybe she had been locked in a tower for years and years (and years), but she had never seen such a bunch of prissy girls in her life! With the single exception of the girl in the muddy gown, the room was filled with nothing but fancy-pants princesses.

Like Rapunzel, all of the girls in this class were at Princess School for the first time. They were first-years,

Bloomers. Girls returning for their second year were known as Sashes. Third-years were Robes, and the fourth and final-year students were called Crowns.

Rapunzel slouched. This bunch of Bloomers looked a little fidgety. Most of them had not taken their seats. They were introducing themselves with small nods and curtsies, exchanging compliments and pleasantries while Rapunzel sat back and chewed the end of her braid. If this was how Princess School was going to be, Rapunzel wasn't sure she could take it.

Rapunzel turned her narrowed eyes toward one of the prettiest Bloomers in the class, Briar Rose. Dressed in a stunning gown that matched her blue eyes, Rose had shining golden hair and a warm smile. She was completely surrounded by other novice princesses. Already they had a nickname for her: "Beauty." Ugh!

"I'll bet she is just full of herself," Rapunzel muttered to a sour-looking king on the tapestry closest to her. "And I bet she couldn't eat her way out of a gingerbread house."

Rapunzel had no respect for people who couldn't take care of themselves. After all, she had been taking care of herself since she was tiny — since Madame Gothel took her from her parents and put her in a thirty-foot tower.

"Nobody keeps me locked up," Rapunzel mumbled, though she had to admit she'd had some help escaping — at least the first time. She was only seven when Val, short for Prince Valerian, appeared at the base of the tower and called up to her.

Rapunzel's scowl disappeared when she thought about her friend. He might be a prince, but he would always be plain old Val to her. Val was eight when he first stumbled across Rapunzel's tower in the woods. He wasn't trying to save her or anything. He just wanted somebody to play with.

"Come down!" he'd called.

"How?" Rapunzel asked.

"Just climb!" he'd answered.

At first Rapunzel thought he was kidding. The tower was almost ten times her height!

"I bet you can't," Val teased.

So then, of course, she did. He coached her, pointing out places to put her hands and feet.

"I would have climbed up," Val said when Rapunzel finally made it to the bottom, "but heights make me vomit."

Rapunzel smiled as she remembered the incredible sense of freedom she'd felt that first time she'd escaped from the tower. Being cooped up was horrible! As the memory faded, Rapunzel saw a girl with silky brown hair and a pink gown curtsy in her direction. In an instant the scowl was back.

Rapunzel wished she were with Val right now. He wasn't very far away — just across the rose garden. Rapunzel was sure second-year Charm School could beat the pantaloons off of first-year Princess School. But she knew she had a better chance of turning into a frog than of getting into the all-boys' school.

Maybe I should have tried the Grimm School, Rapunzel thought as the first-year girls settled into their chairs with a swish of skirts. Glaring at the back of the perfectly postured princess in front of her, Rapunzel knew that would never have worked out, either. The Grimm School was actually closer to her tower than Princess School, but the students who went there were *spooky*. They were real witches! Not only did they learn to fly on broomsticks, which actually sounded kind of fun, they also practiced magic. They concocted potions and cast spells on anything and everything, from trees to animals to people. It was rumored that a few years ago a Grimm girl had even turned a princess into a lizard! And if you thought the students were bad, the teachers were positively evil. Rapunzel shivered. She'd had her fill of nasty sorceresses living with Madame Gothel.

Just then Madame Garabaldi, the Bloomers' hearth-room instructor, strode importantly into the room and held her arms wide for the pages to take her robe. Her silver-streaked hair was pulled into a tight bun, and her hazel eyes gazed sharply over her half-spectacles at the students. Madame Garabaldi cleared her throat as a scribe hurriedly passed scrolls to all the girls. Then, with a final horn blast, class began.

Rapunzel scanned the list of classes written on the silver-leaf-trimmed scroll she'd just received.

Fine Art of Self-defense

That sounded okay.

Frog Identification

Not too terrible.

History: Princesses Past and Present

Well, all right.

Stitchery: Needlework, Spinning, and Embroidery Basics

Were they serious?

Rapunzel gazed down at the scroll to read the final class:

Looking Glass Class — Hairdo How-to and Essential Self-reflection

With a moan, Rapunzel dropped the scroll on her desk and glanced around to see her classmates' reactions. The other Bloomers were gazing politely at Madame Garabaldi, who strode around the chamber, reading from an enormous scroll all of the rules the girls were expected to follow.

"Proper attire is to be worn at all times," Madame

15

Garabaldi enunciated. Her gaze left the list and settled on the barefoot girl who Rapunzel had noticed on the bridge. The girl's face reddened. It didn't look like much got past Madame G.

"Politeness must be observed," Madame Garabaldi rapped out. "Continuously maintain a regal countenance. Homework will be carefully completed. And you must *always* be prompt." Madame Garabaldi laid down the scroll.

"You will find," she continued, "that the punishments we serve here at Princess School are not nearly as harsh as those realities you will encounter once you graduate." Pausing for effect, Madame Garabaldi breathed a puff of air out her nose. She almost looked like a dragon. "Or perhaps you'd have a vine time living the rest of your days as a ridiculously colored squash?" She finished by gazing around the room, smiling at her own joke. But the smile was not exactly warm or welcoming.

Rapunzel stuffed her braid back in her mouth and chewed. Was this what it felt like to be nervous?

Suddenly the heavy classroom doors swung open with a *whoosh*, and the palest princess Rapunzel had ever seen stumbled in.

"Pardon the interruption, Madame Garabaldi," a page said, skirting the girl and bowing low several times before the stern teacher. His hands were shaking slightly. "May I present Snow White?" He gestured toward the pale girl with black hair before backing quickly out of the room, flourishing his pointy hat.

Snow White stood alone at the front of the room. All eyes were on her, and her too-short, high-collared, old-fashioned dress.

Madame Garabaldi was too angry to speak. Her lips quivered and she looked like she wanted to turn Snow White into a pumpkin. Everyone waited for her to say something.

But it was Snow White who spoke first.

Her berry-red lips turned up into a silly grin, and she gave a little wave to all the girls staring at her.

"Hi-ho, everyone!" she chirped.

Rapunzel let her braid drop from her mouth. *Things could be worse*, she thought. *I could be* her.

Chapter Three
Snow White

Snow White smiled at her new classmates. In spite of the scowling woman next to her, her heart was full of joy. She was at Princess School! And she was sure that each and every one of the girls looking at her would become a good friend.

"As it is your first day of Princess School, your tardiness will be excused," Madame Garabaldi said in a carefully controlled voice. It sounded as if her teeth were clenched. "But should it happen again, you will receive double tower detention. Be warned: Tardiness has been the demise of many a princess." The instructor looked pointedly at each girl in the class before turning back to Snow. "Please take your seat," she said in a low tone. "Now."

Snow shivered. The look on Madame Garabaldi's face reminded her of the way her stepmother, easily the most horrible person Snow had ever met, used to look at her over the dinner table. Snow's smile returned. *I don't miss that!* she thought. Surely her new teacher couldn't be as bad as her stepmother.

Snow hummed a little on the way to her seat — a new tune the birds had taught her just that morning. As she turned to sit she caught Madame Garabaldi's eye and the song quickly died in her throat.

Snow did not miss withering looks. Ever since she'd gone to live with her seven surrogates, the dwarves, she hadn't seen anything close to a glare. Until now.

Tomorrow, she told herself, *I'll just have to get up earlier.*

Snow hadn't meant to be late. But she'd needed to help pack seven lunches and see the dwarves off to work. Then she had stopped for a quick visit with Mother Sparrow, whose injured wing Snow was tending. It was almost healed. Snow swung her feet under her desk, thinking of her happy home in the forest.

Behind her, other Bloomers were starting to whisper.

"She doesn't look a thing like a princess! How did she get in?"

"And where did she get that outfit? Look at that collar!"

"I heard she was raised by gnomes."

Snow's feet swung more slowly under her desk. She would not let her good mood be ruined by gossip. She had come too far. She'd even walked past the

Grimm School *by herself* on the way here. She had been looking forward to this for months.

Life with the dwarves was good. Wonderful, even. They worked together to keep their small house tidy. Snow did most of the cooking (though the dwarves often offered to prepare the food, they *all* preferred her delicious soups and pies to their gray gruels and goulashes), but as she worked, the dwarves entertained her with music. And they were constantly doing nice things for Snow, like picking her flowers or bringing her an empty bird's nest. The only bad thing about her cottage life was that the dwarves worked a lot, and Snow got lonely while they were gone . . . even with the company of the woodland animals.

Snow smiled at a few of the girls seated close to her. *They'll like me once they get to know me*, she thought.

A couple of the girls turned away from Snow, but one or two returned her smile, including the friendly-looking, dirty-gowned girl just behind her.

Snow felt better already. Nothing kept her down for long. And look, at the front of the room Madame Garabaldi was reading the school announcements and looking a lot less stern.

"By decree, the Royal Coronation Ball will be held at the end of your second week at Princess School!" she announced. "At the ball, one student — the most elegant and graceful of all — will be crowned Princess of the Ball!" Madame Garabaldi practically beamed. She gazed into the distance and swayed back and forth to imaginary music.

The mood in the room changed at once as everyone pictured herself at the Coronation Ball. The girls began to murmur with excitement. Many of the Bloomers, like Snow White, were born princesses, but lots of them were merely princess hopefuls waiting for an opportunity to wear a crown. This could be their chance.

"The honor of being the Princess of the Ball is great," Madame Garabaldi went on, still smiling and swaying. "It cannot be won by birth or marriage. Indeed not. It is an honor bestowed by one's peers. Every girl in the school will get to cast a vote, and she who is most admired will be crowned."

A few of the princesses glanced expectantly at the beautiful princess with shining, wheat-colored hair and striking blue eyes.

"Of course," Madame Garabaldi continued with a mild look of disdain, "a Bloomer has not received such an honor in more than four dozen years. I certainly would not recommend getting your hopes up."

The excitement in the room faded as quickly as it had grown. Only Snow did not notice the change in the atmosphere. The room was silent when she clapped her hands together, unable to contain her enthusiasm.

"Oh my great golly goodness," she exclaimed. "My very first ball!"

Chapter Four
A Single Slipper

Ella slipped out of hearthroom the moment class ended. It was easy to go unnoticed now. The whole school was abuzz with talk of the ball. Ella made her way through the pink-and-white mazelike hallways, past the gilded, velvet-lined trunks where girls kept their books and supplies, and toward the flower-carved winding staircases leading to other wings of the castle. Around her she heard girls planning what they should wear.

"Do you think rubies go with silk?" a second-year Sash asked her friend as they strolled by, arm in arm.

"Oh, Arabelle! You *have* to wear your tiara," another girl said loudly to a group of her friends. "Have any of you seen it? It is royally gorgeous!"

Talk of ribbons, gowns, and jewels spilled off everyone's tongues. Ella wished she could stop and talk to the other girls. But what would she say? She didn't have a fancy hair ribbon to her name, let alone a gown suitable for a ball.

"At least I can finally get some shoes," Ella consoled herself. Maybe Lurlina could help her out with something to wear to the ball, too. Ella stopped in front of a heavy wooden door and slowly pushed it open. An ornately carved sign over her hand read PRINCESS SCHOOL ROYAL ADMINISTRATIVE CHAMBER.

"I'm looking for Lurlina Busybustle, if you please," Ella said with a curtsy to the woman behind the gilded desk.

"Oh, you must be Ella. Lurly left something for you," the woman said kindly. Then she began pawing through an enormous velvet bag filled with scrolls.

"You mean she's not here?" Ella asked. She felt a lump growing in her throat.

"Oh, no, dear," came the muffled reply from inside the bag. "Aha!" she said, emerging with a small scroll in her hand and a very disheveled hairdo. "Here we are. This should explain everything."

Ella was reaching for the scroll when a rather short page she hadn't even noticed leaped up and grabbed it. He gave the trumpeter by the door a sharp jab with his elbow, and after a few sour notes were played, the page cleared his throat to read.

After a moment of panic Ella calmed herself. "If

you don't mind," she said, putting out her hand, "I'd rather read it myself."

The page handed Ella the note sheepishly. "Of course, your nearly royalness, of course. My mistake," he said with a bow. "It's been such a long summer. I guess I'm anxious to read some decrees."

The page sat back down in the far corner and tilted his hat so it covered his eyes, and Ella began to read.

Halloo Dearie,

I forgot to tell you I am going to a fairy convention in Afaraway Land. I'll be back in three weeks. Sorry I'll miss the Coronation Ball. Have fun in Princess School. I knew you'd get in!

Love,
LB

P.S. Hope you are enjoying the shoes.

Ella's heart sank as she read. Three weeks! She couldn't possibly go barefoot for that long! What was she going to do? Bending her knees so her skirt touched the floor, Ella turned slowly toward the door.

"I have something else for you, too, dear. I think you left this at your interview." The woman behind the desk handed Ella a box. Inside it was one lovely, but oversized, glass shoe.

"Thank you." Ella smiled weakly, remembering the awful interview. She'd had to sit in a much-too-tall chair across from the Dean of Admissions, Miss Prim. And she'd had a terrible time answering the questions because all she could think about the whole time was how to keep her shoes from slipping off and breaking on the stone floor.

When Miss Prim had finally told her she could go, Ella was so anxious to get out of there she accidentally stepped out of one of her shoes. At first she was too embarrassed to go back for it. When she had summoned up her courage to reenter the dean's office, Miss Prim was holding the shoe in her hand, turning it this way and that and gazing at it with what looked like . . . admiration.

Ella couldn't ask for it back after that. Instead, with burning cheeks, she'd pulled off the other shoe, run all the way home, and received a serious lecture from her stepmother for being late. And of course, merciless teasing from Hagatha and Prunilla. Only her father had told her everything would be okay — but he'd told her in a whisper so his wife wouldn't hear. It wasn't particularly reassuring.

Ella gazed at the shoe in her hand. After her interview she'd been certain that the fancy footwear would keep her out of Princess School. Now she wondered if it had gotten her in.

Ella sighed. Little good the shoe would do her now without Lurlina to resize the pair. Ella tried not to think about how she was going to survive for three weeks without her fairy godmother — or what she would wear to the ball.

"Head down, feet covered," she mumbled to herself as she hurried toward her next class. Except for a large group of girls farther down the corridor, the halls were empty and the trunks were closed.

Ella did not want to be late and call attention to herself. But as she approached the group of girls, something made her slow. *Hungch-henh-henh-henh-hungch.* That laugh! Only Prunilla snorted like that when she laughed. And Hagatha's nasal cackle was echoing in the corridor as well.

Hagatha and Prunilla were standing in the center of a bunch of Bloomers Ella recognized from Madame Garabaldi's hearthroom. Ella backed into a doorway. She wasn't ready to deal with her stepsisters at school. Not with Lurlina gone. And not when they were laughing. Only one thing amused Hag and Prune: cruelty.

Ella carefully peeked around the corner to see what they were up to.

"It happens every year," Hagatha hissed at the big-eyed Bloomers. Prunilla nodded beside her sister. "Sometimes the wolf eats the princesses alive and they have to be chopped out. Sometimes he doesn't eat them at all, just chews up their limbs and spits out their bones!"

"Oh, no!" one of the first-years cried.

"How awful!" another shrieked.

The Bloomers pressed closer together. Some of them glanced over their shoulders. Only the girl with the massive, sloppily braided bun — Rapunzel — stood by herself. Her arms were folded across her chest. She didn't look scared but she was definitely listening.

"They come out of the woods and swim the moat." Prunilla made swimming motions with her arms. "They can smell Bloomer blood for miles, you know."

"I've never heard of a wolf that eats young girls!" a cheery voice from the Bloomer crowd protested. It was Snow White.

"These wolves do," Hagatha snapped back. "They're enchanted. The Grimm School sends them." Snow did not protest again.

"But you don't have to take our word for it," Prunilla said in singsong. "You'll see for yourselves soon enough!"

Hagatha and Prunilla pushed their way out of the crowd and sauntered down the hall. Then Hagatha turned quickly and snarled with her teeth bared, looking every bit as awful as a rabid wolf.

The shaken Bloomers screamed in terror and jumped back. All except Rapunzel, who followed the older girls down the hall, watching them with narrowed eyes.

Ella was dumbstruck. She didn't believe Hagatha and Prunilla's stories — not for a second. It was just like them to try to make the new girls scared. What shocked Ella the most was that Hag and Prune were being so terrible to, well, everyone! She always thought they saved their awfulness for her.

The thought of her stepsisters terrorizing her whole class made Ella furious. She wished like never before that she could stand up to them.

Then Ella had a terrible thought. What if everyone at Princess School found out Hagatha and Prunilla were her stepsisters? They might assume she was awful, just like them!

She would have to show the other Bloomers she was on their side. To do that she was going to have to stop going unnoticed. Ignoring her bare feet, Ella strode quickly down the hall. She beckoned to the still-cowering girls.

"Come on!" she called encouragingly. "We don't want to be late for class!"

One of the Bloomers, Snow White, smiled warmly at Ella. The rest of the girls were somber as they pressed together and shakily made their way down the hall.

Chapter Five

Rose

Madame Taffeta's skirts rustled as she gently took Rose's square of muslin and held it up for the rest of the princesses to see. "Note how the stitches are perfectly spaced and sized," she said, her gray eyes wide with admiration. Her round face was rosy from excitement. "Even the choice of thread color is perfect. The mossy green looks positively elegant against the cream muslin! And it's only our second day of classes!"

The girls were in Stitchery class, practicing basic threadwork. They sat in a large circle, each on a comfortable chair with a velvet cushion. Squares of plain muslin, spools of thread, needles, and shiny silver scissors sat on an ornately carved table in the center of the circle. A fire crackled cheerily at one end of the chamber.

Some of the Bloomers looked admiringly at Rose as the teacher held her muslin aloft. But others, including

Rapunzel, openly glared at her. Rose sighed and let her threaded needle fall to her lap, being careful not to let the sharp end touch her finger. Her stitches were straight, even, and perfectly sized, it was true.

Rose had been sewing for as long as she could remember, and with a disadvantage. Whenever Rose went near a needle, her parents forced her to wear a thimble on every finger, for fear she would prick herself. Rose didn't know why. It wasn't easy learning to sew with metal fingertips, but over time Rose had gotten good at it. So now, without those annoying thimbles, her stitching was even better — and she was faster at it. But she wished Madame Taffeta would stop making a fuss.

There was another girl who was fast — the friendly girl who'd been barefoot yesterday — Ella. She moved the needle and thread through the fabric so quickly, it was as if she desperately wanted the task to be done. She had already gone to the table to get a second and a third piece of muslin. Her stitches were almost as even as Rose's, and she had chosen a color that was almost identical to the mossy green. Why didn't Madame Taffeta compliment her?

As if deciding to squash any hope Rose had of ever being normal, Madame Taffeta began to speak again. "Briar Rose, would you like to demonstrate your perfect stitching technique? I'm sure the other girls would benefit greatly from an illustration of your talent."

Rose had no desire to demonstrate anything. For a moment she thought of pointing out Ella's fine stitches. But something stopped her. That first morning on the stairs, Ella had seemed terrified of being noticed. Standing up in front of the whole class might be even worse for her.

Rose stood and quickly ran her needle and thread through the muslin, making a straight line of even stitches.

"Perfect!" Madame Taffeta exclaimed. She snatched up the fabric and held it next to the window so the light shone behind it, making the stitches more visible.

Rose barely glanced at the muslin as she took her seat, but something outside the window caught her eye.

Oh my gosh! she thought, feeling her face flush with embarrassment. Was that Dahlia, one of her guardian fairies, hovering in midair?

The winged pest was spying on her! Rose quickly looked away, hoping Dahlia would disappear before anyone else saw her. That's when she noticed that Rapunzel was glaring at her for the second time in ten minutes. This time, Rose was ready. She glared right back. It wasn't as if she *asked* for this attention. Rapunzel's eyes widened in surprise before she lowered them back to her stitching.

Rose blew out her breath. Being so blessed and so protected was driving her crazy!

I wouldn't even mind being teased by the older girls! Rose thought desperately. Most of the Bloomers were miserable and terrified, and for good reason. The first day and a half of school had been grueling, and not just because of the rules and coursework. Terrible things had been happening to them!

First there was that horrible story about a cursed Grimm wolf eating the first-years. Rose wasn't sure she believed it, but the idea was enough to make anyone shiver. Then there were the trippings. An innocent Bloomer would be hurrying off to class when — *WHAM!* — she would suddenly find herself and whatever she was carrying sprawled across the cold stone floor. A few of the third-year Robes forced the new girls to guess their names, not letting them pass in the hall until they did so successfully. This usually made the Bloomers late for class, which got them in big trouble. But even tower detention (the punishment for being tardy) was not as humiliating as the drenchings. Some nasty Crowns rigged buckets of icy water over the trunks of unsuspecting Bloomers, soaking the girls as soon as the lids were lifted. Wet and shivering, the Bloomers would have to maintain their composure and dignity while they dried off as best they could and rushed off to wherever they had to go next.

Rose shuddered as she remembered that morning's drenching. It was early, and the sun had not yet peeked out from behind the clouds to warm the castle. The girl was small and had shivered uncontrollably as she made her way to class. Rose had wanted to go over and help the girl, but just then a group of Bloomers had come over to ask Rose what she was going to wear to the ball. Before she could break away, the cold and dripping girl was gone.

I'd like to do something about those cruel tricks, Rose thought. *Why can't the older girls just leave us alone?*

Except, of course, they *were* leaving Rose alone. She was getting the usual special treatment. And that was part of the problem!

The Self-defense class chamber was a giant room nearly as big as the school's stables. Thick, woven wool rugs covered the floor. There was no furniture, but today the room was decorated with large wooden props painted to look like trees and shrubs. The chamber looked like a forest.

The Bloomers stood in small groups waiting for Madame Lightfoot to give them instructions. Madame

Lightfoot was famous, the first princess in the land trained in the art of royal self-defense. Though she was the oldest teacher at Princess School, her braided gray hair was the only sign of her age. She was tall and stood so straight that her presence alone was intimidating. She was strict and did not tolerate students who did not work hard on their defense skills but her smile was never far below the surface.

Rose was eyeing the clusters of girls sprinkled throughout the room when Snow White skipped over. "I just loved your stitches!" Snow exclaimed. "If I could sew like that, the dwarves' clothes would almost never need mending. I swear I spend half my days restitching the same tears!" She let out a small giggle.

Rose had to smile. At least the pale girl's compliments were unique! "Do you really live with dwarves?" she asked, intrigued.

"Oh, yes!" Snow answered. "Seven of them! They are the funniest little men — a little strange at first, but really lovable once you get to know them. They bring me flowers and sing merry songs. Oh, and they protect me from —"

Just then Madame Lightfoot clapped her hands to get the girls' attention.

"Today we will be practicing the woodland-path-skip-trip," she announced. She moved swiftly around the room, pairing up the princesses. Rose was hoping she would be paired with Snow so she could learn more about the dwarves (like, how small were they? And would they be interested in meeting a bunch of fairies with too much free time?) but was not so lucky. Snow was paired with Ella. And Rose was paired with Rapunzel — the girl with the ridiculously long auburn hair and the mean stare.

Rapunzel gave a little snort when Madame Lightfoot pulled her and Rose together. The gleam in her eye was mischievous.

She looks like she wants to make a noose out of that hair and string me up, Rose thought. But she didn't care, and she wasn't afraid. It actually felt kind of nice to be scoffed at!

Madame Lightfoot went on, "This tactic is especially good when you find a devilish witch, wolf, or other beast of no-good nature sneaking up to devour you."

There was a chorus of shrieks, doubtless because of the rumored Grimm School wolf. Did Madame Lightfoot know about it? Rose wondered. Was that why she was teaching this skill during the first week of class?

"Ladies," the instructor said sternly, "we are here to learn to defend ourselves. Not to squeal and shriek like helpless children!"

The Bloomers quieted, and Madame Lightfoot continued. "Now, to begin the skip-trip, you must get into a good skipping rhythm. Whenever you are skipping through the forest, of course, you must continuously look from side to side for potential attackers. Keep your basket pushed back to your elbow so your hands are free. Then, when you see someone or something suspicious approaching you, throw out your forward skipping foot to knock the perpetrator off balance. That accomplished, grab your attacker around the neck and toss the scoundrel to the ground. It's really quite simple."

"It sounds mean!" Rose overheard Snow whispering to Ella. She watched as the shabbily dressed girl patted Snow's arm reassuringly. They had to be the nicest pair in the class!

Madame Lightfoot gazed around the chamber at the faces of the confused princesses. "Perhaps a demonstration," she said. "May I have a volunteer to be the scoundrel I am to trip?"

Rose was about to volunteer — maybe it would show the other girls that she didn't think she was too good to land flat on her face — when Rapunzel stepped forward. Madame Lightfoot immediately began to skip in slow motion. Rapunzel assumed a skulking pose and half-hid behind one of the wooden trees. She looked like she was just about to lunge at Madame Lightfoot when the teacher kicked her right foot to the side, knocking Rapunzel's left foot and throwing her off balance. An instant later, Madame Lightfoot tossed

Rapunzel over her shoulder and onto the soft green carpet like a small bale of hay. *Thud!* Rapunzel landed flat on her back.

Rapunzel beamed and leaped to her feet. "Incredible!" she said, not sounding very princesslike. Rose had to admire the girl's attitude. Would she have been as relaxed?

It didn't take long to find out. Madame Lightfoot instructed them to begin working in their pairs at once, and Rapunzel began skipping away. Rose lunged gracefully, but Rapunzel tripped her and tossed her to the ground like a sack of wet wool.

"Are you all right, Princess?" Rapunzel asked. Her voice was not entirely sincere, but Rose pretended not to notice.

"I'm fine," she replied pleasantly, getting to her feet.

Beside them, Snow and Ella were negotiating their own skip-trip. Ella was skipping and Snow was tripping — or, at least, she was trying to. As Ella approached, she slowed down, afraid to trod on Snow's foot. Snow kicked out her leg, but then threw out her hand to keep Ella from falling. Ella grabbed Snow's hand and sat down with a bump.

"Oops!" Ella giggled. "Maybe we should try that again. You don't have to be so nice, you know."

"Sorry," Snow apologized.

Those two are well matched, Rose thought. Then she

looked back at her own partner. She was well matched, too, she decided. Without even dusting herself off, Rose began her own skip, casting her eyes in all directions. Rapunzel came at her from behind a bush, but Rose was ready. She kicked out a leg with lightning speed and hurled Rapunzel to the ground so fast the girl got the wind knocked out of her.

Rose felt a little guilty. She hadn't meant to trip Rapunzel that hard. She was about to apologize when Rapunzel looked up, a wide grin on her face.

"Nice one!" she complimented Rose as she got to her feet and regained her breath. "Can you show me how to do it that fast?"

Rose grinned back. She had a sneaking suspicion she'd just made a friend. And not because she was pretty!

"Of course!" she replied.

Chapter Six
Step-by-step

Ella filled a platter with roasted meat and vegetables and hurried out to the dining room. She didn't want to listen to her stepmother or stepsisters complain about how slow she was. Or how lazy. Or how stupid. She was feeling deflated as it was.

It seemed that in the two days since she'd started Princess School, her stepsisters were more determined than ever to keep her swamped with chores at home. Suddenly the meals she had to prepare had seven courses instead of five. The mending basket was always overflowing. Hagatha and Prunilla had dirtied an extra gown a day, nearly doubling her laundry chores. Just yesterday they put in their winter furs to be aired, and it wasn't even October!

As Ella served the meat and vegetables, she tried not to look too tired. The more tired she appeared, the more her sisters ridiculed her.

"Everyone's talking about the Royal Coronation Ball at school, Mother," Prunilla said as she pecked at a scrap of meat. She looked scornfully at Ella holding the platter of food. "The meat is underseasoned again," she snapped. "Bring me the salt."

"You would think she would learn from her mistakes," Kastrid said coolly. "And yet we have to tell her again and again."

Ella knew the meat was seasoned perfectly. Besides, if she'd added any more salt, her stepsisters would complain that it was oversalted. She just couldn't win. Not since her father had married Kastrid.

"I think the meat is just right," Ella thought she heard her father murmur. She was standing right next to him with the platter. But if anyone else heard, they did not respond. With an aching heart, Ella wished her mother were still alive. How different things would be!

Ella sighed silently and handed Prunilla the glass bowl of salt that sat on the table, well within her reach. Her stepsisters never did anything for themselves if they could make Ella do it for them.

"Anyway," Prunilla said, casting a sideways glance at Ella, "they say the ball is going to be grander than ever this year. The ballroom floor is going to be repolished and the orchestra will have a dozen extra musicians! The fourth-year Crowns are in charge of decorating the ballroom, of course, but Headmistress

Bathilde has asked me to help decorate the ballot box!"

"You!" Hagatha cried, her eyes flashing with envy. "What about me?"

"Well, she asked *me*. But I suppose if you let me borrow your brocade cape I might let you help," Prunilla said coyly.

Hagatha scowled. "I was going to wear that cape, and you know it!" she howled.

"Girls, girls," Ella's stepmother said. "Let's not argue. Of course your sister will let you help with the ballot box," she told Hagatha. "And both of you will be beautifully dressed for the occasion."

"I'm sure all three of you girls will have a wonderful time at the ball," Ella's father added quietly.

The room fell silent, and for a moment Ella was grateful that her father had spoken up for her. But one glance at her stepmother's narrowing eyes told her she shouldn't be. The look on Kastrid's face was so cruel that Ella almost dropped the basket of bread she was holding.

"Ella is lucky to be attending Princess School at all," Kastrid snapped. "It has yet to be seen whether she deserves to go to the ball as well."

Ella looked over at her father, hoping he would say something else. His eyes flitted between his plate of food and his wife's angry face.

"But the ball is for all Princess School students, is it not, my sweet?" he said, almost in a whisper.

Kastrid slammed her wine goblet down on the table so hard that the red liquid spilled onto the white lace tablecloth — another stain for Ella to remove.

"We shall discuss this later, *darling*," Ella's stepmother declared, giving Ella's father a withering look. As Ella returned to the kitchen to finish preparing the dessert, her heart went out to her father. Being married to Kastrid could not be any easier than having her for a stepmother. And she knew he had married her because he thought she, his only child, needed a mother.

There was no mention of the ball during the rest of the meal. But as soon as Ella had cleared the dishes and filled the sink with hot water, her stepsisters flounced into the kitchen, talking loudly about the ball.

"I want all of my gowns cleaned and pressed so I can try them on and choose the one that makes me look prettiest," Prunilla announced.

"And I want each and every piece of my gold and silver jewelry polished to a perfect shine so I can choose the ones that bring out my eyes," Hagatha added.

Ella wanted to tell Hagatha that her beady eyes

were not her best asset. Why bring them out? And nothing could make Prunilla pretty, since her heart was as black as coal. But Ella said nothing, only continued washing the giant pile of dishes next to the stone sink.

"We're so sorry you won't be coming to the ball with us," Hagatha said in a sugary-sweet voice.

"Yes," Prunilla agreed. Her face contorted into a sneer. "Who will fetch our refreshments and adjust the skirts of our gowns?"

Ella gritted her teeth. *Politeness must be observed*, she told herself, repeating Madame Garabaldi's words. Somehow they fell flat. Still, Ella said nothing.

Then Hagatha's eyes glimmered, and she leaned back. Before Ella knew what was happening the soup tureen fell to the floor, smashing and splattering soup everywhere, especially all over Ella. Her stepsisters, of course, leaped out of the way just in time.

"What a mess!" Prunilla said. "You are as clumsy as you are slow!"

"You'd better clean it up before Mother finds out you broke her best tureen," Hagatha added.

Cackling like a pair of court jesters, the two left Ella alone in the kitchen with porcelain shards and spattered vegetable soup.

Ella held back tears as she got down on her hands

and knees to begin cleaning up the mess. As she sopped up the soup with a rag, she accidentally cut her hand on a broken tureen shard. In an instant her sadness disappeared, and she was filled with anger.

"I *will* go to the ball," she said aloud between gritted teeth. "And *not* to fetch cakes or adjust skirts!"

Chapter Seven

Mirror, Mirror

Rapunzel sighed. Looking Glass class was turning out to be as awful as she'd feared. Perching on a small velvet stool in front of a dressing table with a huge mirror was bad enough. Rapunzel didn't think she was much to look at, and staring at herself in the mirror only seemed to prove that she was right. Her freckled nose was straight. Her eyes weren't crossed or anything. And Rapunzel had always loved her hair — it was original and incredibly handy.

But in Looking Glass class, in addition to having to look at herself for more than an hour (boring), she was expected to weave fancy braids and twist curls and place hair clips just so. Rapunzel eyed the brush, comb, ribbons, hair clips, and curling iron in front of her. She was sure they would be of no help in tackling her untamable tresses.

Rapunzel held up a thick reddish-brown lock, eyeing it doubtfully. At the dressing table next to her,

Rose smiled encouragingly. "Just divide it into sections and weave them together," she said.

"Easy for you to say," Rapunzel replied, smirking. "Your hair doesn't resemble a ship's riggings!"

Rose giggled and continued to weave her golden tresses into a French braid. She didn't even have to pay attention to what she was doing. Instead, she was listening to the girl on the other side of her prattle on about the ball.

"I hear the crown is made of glittering diamonds!" the girl said, her blue eyes reflecting wide in the looking glass.

"I thought it was made of rubies," Rose replied.

"Someone told me it's made of both!" a third student said. "And sapphires, too!" A chorus of oohs echoed in the chamber.

"I hope a prince asks me to dance!" one of the Bloomers blurted out.

Suddenly the room filled with chatter about the Charm School for Boys. Everyone was giggling, and several girls blushed as well. Besides Rapunzel, only Ella was quiet. She seemed almost sullen as she combed and recombed the same lock of hair.

"I can't wait," said Snow White. "I've been practicing my dancing with the woodland animals."

"I hear the princes at Charm School are majestically cute!" another princess chimed in.

Rapunzel snorted. What was the big deal about boys? They were like girls, really — only different. She and Val had been friends for years, and he didn't make her blush or giggle — more like belly laugh — and he was a boy.

For the millionth time, Rapunzel wished she were with Val instead of stuck at Princess School. Charm School was probably a blast!

While I'm here primping Val gets to fence and gallop on horseback! she thought miserably. *He's right on the other side of the gardens, and I never even see him!*

"Ah, girls," Madame Spiegel said, pulling Rapunzel out of her thoughts. The teacher was standing next to her dressing table at the front of the room, gazing at her own reflection, which was lovely. The young teacher had long, wavy blond hair, strikingly high cheekbones, and wide-set brown eyes.

"You can never be sure what will be reflected back at you when you look in a mirror," she said mysteriously. She caught Rapunzel's eyes in the looking glass. "Can you see your true self?"

Rapunzel made a face at herself and her hopelessly messy hair in the mirror. Of course she saw herself. Who else would she see?

Suddenly one of the girls — the tiny one who had gotten soaked by a bucket of freezing water the day before — leaped up off her stool with a shriek.

"Madame Spiegel," she cried. "I think there's something under my seat!" The poor girl had been moaning and twisting uncomfortably on her stool all morning. Rapunzel thought it was because she had caught a chill from the drenching. Now, she realized, it could be much worse.

The room went silent. The princesses' eyes widened. It couldn't be . . .

Without a word, Madame Spiegel went over to the princess's stool. Slowly and carefully she helped the girl remove cushion after cushion from her seat. Since the girl was so small, she had at least half a dozen piled on her chair.

The rest of the Bloomers exchanged silent glances while they held their breath, waiting to see what the lump was. Rapunzel hoped it was just a piece of batting that had gathered together inside one of the cushions. The other possibility was too horrible. Too cruel.

Finally Madame Spiegel lifted the last cushion from the girl's stool. There, slightly squashed but still intact, was a single pea.

At once the chamber was filled with cries of disbelief.

"A pea! A pea!" someone screamed.

"I don't believe it," another girl cried.

The princess who had been sitting on the pea fell to the floor in a faint.

Rapunzel felt sorry for the girl. Personally, she was not afraid of peas — she was pretty confident she could sit on one for hours and barely notice. But peas had sent several princesses into tailspins — robbing them of sleep, making it impossible for them to sit or lie down for days — some pea victims had even needed medical attention. Needless to say, most princesses were terrified of them. Rapunzel would never use the small round vegetable against another princess, not even a princess she didn't like. It was an unspoken rule — a princess pact.

"Who would do such an awful thing?" Rose said aloud as several girls gathered around the fallen princess.

"I have an idea," Rapunzel heard Ella say under her breath so quietly that Rapunzel was quite sure nobody else heard.

"Girls, we must remain calm." Madame Spiegel's voice was steady but strained. "Panic helps no princess." She crouched down over the princess who had fainted and held a small jar of smelling salts under her nose. The girl opened her eyes.

The tiny worry lines that had creased the teacher's flawless skin disappeared. "We must have courage and faith in ourselves," she said. "Without those things we will be defeated by unkind tricks such as these."

Madame Spiegel helped the victimized princess to

her feet, removed the pea from the stool, and set the cushions back on top.

Holding the offending pea at arm's length like a soiled diaper, Madame Spiegel ceremoniously carried the pea to the hearth and threw it directly onto the embers. The flames shot up and the pea exploded into several pieces before sizzling and disappearing into ashes. "Back to our looking glasses, ladies," she called.

Satisfied the offending vegetable had been properly disposed of, the girls sat back down on their stools, many of them checking for peas first.

Rapunzel watched Madame Spiegel stare at herself in a mirror. Then she turned back to her own reflection and wrestled once more with her unwieldy locks. A plain braid would be easy. But a French braid required small sections of hair — at least at first. And none of the clips on the dressing table looked remotely big enough for even a few strands of her thick hair.

Frustrated, Rapunzel grabbed the hot iron and began to wrap a piece of hair around it. But the iron was heavier than she expected, and she nearly burned her neck.

Just then another face appeared in Rapunzel's looking glass. It was Rose. Her hair had been neatly woven into three French braids, the ends of which were twisted into a neat bun at the nape of her slender neck.

"I hate those things," Rose whispered, pointing to the hot iron. "But I can show you a couple of braiding tricks."

"Great," Rapunzel said, smiling. She sat back, letting Rose take over. Obviously the girl knew what she was doing when it came to hair — just like she did in Self-defense. A few minutes later, Rose had half of the hair in a braid that ran partway down Rapunzel's back.

Grateful, Rapunzel turned her head to look at the sides. A beam of sunlight flashed on the mirror's surface. A second later it happened again. And again.

That's weird, Rapunzel thought. She had already put down her hand mirror. She glanced around the chamber and noticed that nobody else was using a small looking glass, either.

Flash. There it was again. She and Rose exchanged a glance in the mirror above her dressing table, and Rapunzel leaned over to look out the window. Halfway across the garden, she saw a boy standing outside the Princess School stables. Val! He was holding a piece of shiny metal, moving it back and forth so it reflected a beam of light into the Looking Glass chamber window!

"Who is that?" Rose whispered, leaning forward to get a better look.

"My friend Val," Rapunzel replied, waving at him. "He goes to the Charm School."

Rose nodded, looking impressed.

Val flashed his metal again and pointed toward the stables. Rapunzel grinned. Val had thought of the perfect meeting spot and signal!

Chapter Eight

Warts and All

Ella walked down the hall lost in thought. She was tired and shaken. The pea incident played again and again in her head. She was certain Hagatha and Prunilla were behind it — even if they didn't carry out the horrible deed alone. And for some reason their cruelties seemed especially harsh to Ella lately. Maybe it was because she had never seen her stepsisters terrorize other girls. Or maybe it was because she had seen true kindness in some of her teachers and classmates.

Ella's thoughts were interrupted as Snow skipped up beside her, humming a little tune. Looping her arm through Ella's, Snow pulled her toward their next class: Frog Identification.

"Aren't you excited?" Snow asked. "This is my favorite class. And today we get to work with real frogs!"

Snow's enthusiasm was infectious. Ella allowed Snow

to pull her along and felt her spirits being slowly lifted by the cheerful chatter.

"Of course I love Princess School," Snow babbled, "but I do miss the forest animals. They visit me every day when I'm home at the cottage. They don't talk much, but they're wonderful company! Have you ever spent time with a toad? I have. Frogs and toads aren't nearly as cuddly as deer and rabbits and squirrels. But I think they're just as cute — in a slippery sort of way! Don't you agree?"

Ella smiled and nodded. She didn't really find frogs appealing, but she did feel better.

They were almost at the Frog ID chamber door when a group of older princesses began to crowd around them and the rest of the Bloomers, shouting taunts. Ella saw her stepsisters in the middle of the hecklers and ducked her head.

"Watch out for warts!" Prunilla called.

"Careful, girls, don't get slime all over your gowns!" a Sash yelled.

"The poor Bloomers," teased Hagatha. "Where else but in frog class would they get dates for the ball?"

The hall was filled with taunting laughter, but Ella ignored it as Snow led her and the Bloomers into the frog chamber. It was the plainest room in the castle. A fireplace stood at each end to warm the rug-free space. A single row of simple wooden tables ran along one wall. Small cages were lined up on the tables, each one containing a captured frog.

"Step inside, girls," Madame Bultad called. "Contrary to Princess School rumor, there's nothing to be afraid of here."

The girls entered the chamber but stood in a group near the door — all except Snow, who immediately went over to the frog cages to say hello.

Madame Bultad, a squat woman with a broad face and almost-black eyes, cleared her throat. Ella thought the sound was remarkably similar to a croak!

"I know Frog ID is the subject of much ridicule," the teacher said. "But as I've told you before, the skills you are acquiring in this room are essential for every princess." She paused for effect. "Unless you would like to find yourself plagued by a frog that you are unable to identify as either a prince under a spell or a green-skinned trickster."

The girls peered nervously at the caged frogs, whispering to one another. Nobody liked to talk about frogs — they generally made princesses nervous. Ella didn't really mind them. She was used to seeing them at the pond near her home and occasionally in the kitchen garden where she grew vegetables.

Madame Bultad continued, "As we discussed, ordinary frogs have become very skilled at disguising themselves as the real thing in the hopes of being kissed by a princess . . . or a princess-in-training." She sprung open the latch of one of the cages and a large, shiny green frog hopped out. Madame Bultad picked it up with a graceful swoop of her arm.

"Notice the golden-hued warts that cover this frog's body."

"He's beautiful!" Snow cried, rushing forward to get a better look.

Ella couldn't help but smile. But Madame Bultad's face grew serious. "Perhaps, but looks can be deceiving. A decade ago these golden warts would have been a sure sign that this creature is actually a prince under an evil spell. But today's amphibians have cleverly adopted these false clues to fool the inexperienced princess. One out of every five ordinary frogs and toads will have golden warts, spots in a crown configuration on its head, or a similar feature. My advice is this: Do not act in haste. Look carefully. Study your subjects. Only then will you find a prince among frogs."

Madame Bultad smiled, and the frogs began to croak loudly.

"And now, ladies, it is time to release the frogs. Each of you shall step forward and open a cage."

While most of the girls looked at one another in disgust, Snow bounded forward and opened a cage, freeing a frog. Ella stepped up behind her and cau-

tiously lifted a latch. She had never touched a frog before, but they couldn't be *that* bad.

"They're not wolves," Rapunzel called, echoing
Ella's thoughts and stepping forward herself. "They're
frogs!" She sprung a latch and a skinny frog leaped
straight to the floor.

Soon the entire chamber was filled with hopping,
croaking frogs. Ella had never seen so many amphibians in so many shapes and sizes. And many of them
were quite clever. One actually winked at her!

Most of the princesses, though, were not amused —
or even interested. Most of them screamed and tried
to get away when a slimy green hopper drew near.

Ella studied a frog with a silver circle on top of its
head. It was sort of sweet, but . . . slimy.

On the other side of the room, Rose moved gra-
ciously away from a dozen frogs that were all trying
madly to get close to her.

Rapunzel, for her part, sat on the floor nearby talking very calmly to a particularly large, lumpy frog. "It's
nice to see you again, Warty," she said. "And I'm sorry
you've been captured. But I don't care how many hopping contests you've won for me — I'm not going to
kiss you again!"

Just then, Rose calmly strode over, still being followed by at least twelve frogs. "Yech," she said in a very

unprincesslike manner. "I don't care if you *are* under a curse. I'm not going to kiss any of you!" The frogs stopped hopping and croaking and just looked up at Rose, pouting.

Rose looked to Rapunzel for help, but Snow was first to speak. "Don't listen to them," she said, making a hammock in the skirt of her gown to gather up the frogs. "I'll kiss all of you, even if you aren't princes." The frogs hopped excitedly toward her.

"Or will that get me in trouble?" Snow turned to Ella.

Ella abandoned the frog with the silver circle and cautiously reached a finger out to pet one of the frogs in Snow's skirt. "Here, froggy, froggy," she said in a croaky voice. She softly stroked a lumpy frog's back. He actually wasn't as slippery as he looked!

Standing next to them, Rose giggled. The frog Ella was petting croaked loudly, and Ella laughed, too. Warty croaked next and hopped over to Snow. But he was so fat he couldn't jump high enough to get into her skirt-hammock.

"Here you go, Warty," Rapunzel said, giving him a little lift. "You've been putting away the mayflies, haven't you?" The frog flipped right over, letting out a long croak as he landed on the soft fabric of Snow's gown.

"You're welcome," Rapunzel said, laughing.

The next thing they knew, all four girls were giggling hysterically. Across the room, Madame Bultad opened her mouth to tell the girls to be quiet, but began to cough instead.

"Frog in her throat," Rose whispered. Ella and the other girls nearly fell to the floor laughing. They couldn't stop. Ella felt all of her fear and worry slipping away. Frog ID was turning out to be the best class so far!

Then, all of a sudden, the laughter was cut short. Screams from the hall filled the room. "A wolf! A wolf!"

Chapter Nine
Who's Afraid?

A dark-haired Bloomer who had just been to the little princesses' room burst back into Frog ID screaming, "There's a wolf in the hall!"

Leaving the classroom door standing wide open, the girl dashed for the high windows at the back of the room. In a split second her panic spread. Pandemonium broke out.

The loud ribbiting of frightened frogs was overwhelmed by the shrieks of even more frightened princesses. Frogs tripped over one another, trying to get back to the safety of their cages. Bloomers scrambled onto tables, trying to avoid the frogs and reach the high diamond-paned windows. Everyone's worst nightmare had come true. There was a wolf loose in the school.

Strangely, Briar Rose felt calm. She was rarely afraid, but maybe that was because everyone was usually so scared for her she didn't have to be. She moved toward the door, intending to close it and protect the others.

Out in the hall Rose heard another cry. "Help!" A Bloomer in a red cloak dashed past Rose. Chasing after the girl — and moving fast — was a flash of black fur. Rose heard a growl, or maybe a snort, before the chorus of screams behind her drowned out all other noise.

"Is that the wolf?" Snow pushed past Rose into the hallway. The wolf stopped running and stood its ground at the end of the hall. "Oh, isn't he sweet?" Snow crooned, taking a few steps toward the animal with her hand outstretched.

"Shouldn't we grab her?" Rapunzel was suddenly standing behind Rose. Ella was there, too. Madame Bultad, for her part, had hopped up on the tables with the rest of the Bloomers. Her bog-green skirts were hoisted to her knees, showing plenty of yellow stocking.

Before her new friends could pull Snow back inside the room, the wolf turned and ran awkwardly away. It looked as if its two front legs were stunted, and its fur was awfully loose.

A minute later Snow came back into the room. "It's gone!" she called to everyone on the tables, including the teacher. "Poor thing. He looked just awful!"

Rose smiled. Leave it to Snow to be worried about the invader!

Madame Bultad climbed off the table, crossed the room, and cautiously poked her head out the door. Then she cleared her throat. "All clear, girls," she said in her rumbling voice. "Now, stay together and get to your hearthroom while I report this to the administrative chambers!"

The Bloomers held hands and hurried past Rose, looking both ways. Some of them skipped, ready to try their skip-trip if necessary. All of them appeared frazzled. Even Snow.

"I think there was something wrong with that wolf," Snow said, turning back toward her friends, who were still standing by the door. Her voice was full of concern and her eyes were starting to well up with tears.

"I *know* there was," Ella replied over Rose's shoulder. Snow looked like she thought the wolf was hurt, but there was something in Ella's voice that let Rose know Ella was thinking along the same lines she was.

"To start with, that was no wolf," Rose said. She held out her hand to comfort Snow.

Ella nodded. "No. I've seen that fur before, and it doesn't belong to a wolf. It belongs to something worse — my stepmother."

"What do you mean?" Snow's dark eyes sparkled.

Rapunzel pushed a lock of black hair off Snow's porcelain face. Rose had felt like doing the same thing. There was something about Snow. She was so trusting, it made you want to take care of her.

"That was no wolf," Rose announced. "That was a person in a wolf costume."

"Hagatha . . . or Prunilla, one of my stepsisters," Ella added. She wrapped her arm around Snow and glared at the spot where the "wolf" had been. "Those girls live to torture others. I just wish we could prove it was —"

Suddenly Ella stopped talking.

All of the Bloomers had gone, but now a Robe stood in the hallway. She was dressed in a gorgeous sunset-orange dress and her jewels were lovely, but they looked out of place beside the sneer on her face.

"Hey, Cinder Blockhead," Prunilla spat at Ella. "I see you made a new friend." She gestured toward Snow, looking her up and down, obviously disapproving of her old-fashioned dress. "She's perfect for you."

"Leave us alone, Prunilla," Ella said softly.

Prunilla acted like she didn't hear Ella. She slowly walked closer to Snow, staring into her wide eyes. "Do you always look so stupid?" she said with disdain, screwing up her face even more.

"Oh, no," Snow answered sweetly. "I was just so worried about that poor wolf —"

"Never mind," Prunilla cut Snow off and her dark eyes settled on Rose.

Rose watched as Prunilla's whole face changed. She still wasn't what Rose would call beautiful, but the snarl was gone. Now her tiny lips turned up in a smile.

"Briar Rose!" she said in a sickeningly sweet voice. "I'm sure you must have better things to do than to waste your time with this pair of dirty Bloomers! We are reflected in the company we keep, you know. Why don't you come with me, Beauty? I can introduce you to some of the Robes. We usually don't associate with the younger girls, but for you we might make an exception." Prunilla extended her hand limply.

"Thank you. No," Rose replied coolly, stepping closer to Ella, Snow, and Rapunzel and giving Prunilla a steely look. "I don't think I could bear to see myself reflected in *your* shallow eyes."

Prunilla's mouth dropped open into a perfect "O." For a moment she did nothing, then her eyes narrowed into tiny slits. Her mouth closed and opened again. But she was silent as she turned on her heel and stomped away in a huff.

Suddenly Ella bent over, clutching her stomach. Her head bobbed and she gasped for breath. Rose put her hand to her mouth. She hoped she hadn't gotten Ella into trouble! Maybe she shouldn't have said anything to the nasty older girl.

"I'm sorry. Was I out of line?" Rose began.

Ella stood up. Her face was red and tears were running down her cheeks. But she was grinning from ear to ear.

"You might live to regret that," Ella gasped, still trying to control her laughter. "But if you ask me, it was worth it!"

Chapter Ten
Rapunzel's Surprise

Rapunzel ran down the hall as fast as she could. It felt good — no, great — not to worry about regal countenance and posture and poise and . . . UGH!

Because of the wolf scare, all of the princesses had been escorted from their hearthrooms to the far courtyard — away from the Grimm School woods — while the royal guards checked the halls. Rapunzel headed to the other side of the castle, toward the stables and Val. It was the perfect opportunity for her to slip away.

Racing out the front of the school, Rapunzel dashed down the steps and hopped the low wall separating the entrance from the rose garden. She ducked through the prickly bushes and sprinted the last few yards. She hoped Val would still be there. They had arranged to meet in the stables during lunch. The only problem was, Val's lunch ended just as Rapunzel's began.

"Don't worry. Nobody can keep me in," she'd told him. "Just be there." She had sounded confident, but if it hadn't been for this wolf scare, she didn't know how she would have made it in time.

"Val!" Rapunzel called as she flew into the enormous stables. Doves scattered, flying up to the rafters. The horses snorted and pawed the straw at the disturbance. Luckily, none of the stable hands were there. Rapunzel suddenly realized that she could get herself in trouble for being out of school if she was caught.

"Come out, come out, wherever you are," Rapunzel called more quietly. Val *had* to be there. She had stayed up late every night for three nights making him a surprise. She had wanted to give it to him that morning, but he'd left for school early — without her. She simply could not wait another second.

All Rapunzel heard were stomping feet.

Sinking down onto a bale of hay, Rapunzel pulled the surprise out of the pocket she'd stitched into her dress. It was a belt buckle. The buckle had been her father's. Or at least she assumed it had been. It was on the belt Madame Gothel had used to tie up all of her baby things when she whisked Rapunzel away from her parents. Only the buckle had never shone like it did now.

Rapunzel had spent hours polishing and polishing it for Val. She hoped he would wear it every day. That way he would always be ready to flash her messages from the Charm School. Now the buckle was as shiny as her looking glass. Almost. Rapunzel's reflection distorted in the metal and she stuck out her tongue. Wow. And she thought she looked funny in a regular mirror!

"I thought you said you weren't going to turn all prissy and vain on me." Val's laughing voice was muffled in the dim stable. But his smiling green eyes were unmistakable in the shafted light. "And here I find you gazing at yourself in anything that will cast a reflection! Maybe I should start calling *you* 'Beauty.'"

"Oh, stop!" Rapunzel threw the buckle at Val, who stopped teasing long enough to catch it. She felt a pang of guilt for telling Val about Rose's silly nickname, especially now that she really kind of liked the pretty princess. Rose was more than a lovely face. Much more. In fact, she might even be a great friend. But Rapunzel wasn't ready to tell Val about that now. She had other things to tell him about, like the buckle and her plan.

"What's this?" Val asked, turning over the shiny metal object and polishing it a little on his shirt.

"A suit of armor," Rapunzel said dryly. "What do you think?"

Val gave her a look and Rapunzel pulled the rest of her surprise out of her pocket. "*That* is so you can send me light signals when I'm in class on the north side of the building." She pointed at the buckle. "*This*," she said, handing him a small scroll, "is the start of our code."

Rapunzel had come up with several flash sequences that would allow her to communicate with Val. There wasn't too much you could say with light and mirrors. "Hello." "See you later." "Madame Spiegel has a nose like a toadstool." And the most important: "Meet me at the stables — quick!" Rapunzel and Val couldn't exactly have conversations, but it was enough to keep them connected and keep Rapunzel from feeling trapped at Princess School. Besides, once they got good at using it, the code could be expanded.

Val smiled. "What a waste. There you are learning how to do cross-stitch when you would do the most good in King Westerly's Secret Service."

"Hey, I've learned some defensive skills, too." Rapunzel feigned a skip-trip and Val backed away with his hands up.

"Mercy, Your Highness," he said with a bow. "I've heard all about how you can take down pretty girls." Val flopped back in the hay, stretching his long skinny legs. "How *is* Beauty, anyway?" he asked. His eyes twinkled.

"Don't tell me you're stuck on her, too." Rapunzel

knocked the prince's thin crown so it sat askew in his dark curly hair.

"Not stuck, just curious." Val shrugged. "What's she like? Is she just like the stories say?"

It was Rapunzel's turn to shrug. "She's okay." Funny. Last week Rapunzel had been enjoying telling Val all about the fancy frou-frou girls at Princess School and having a good laugh. But now she felt different. Some of the girls weren't so silly. Like when Snow had walked up to that wolf, or whatever it was. That was brave.

Things were changing. Rapunzel didn't feel good about poking fun at the princesses and she didn't know how to explain it to Val. Maybe she was making new friends. Maybe she was fitting in.

Suddenly Rapunzel wanted to get back to school, to see if she was missing anything. The "wolf" could come back at any time!

"So, send me a signal when you're in Chivalry," she said, standing up quickly and backing out of the stables.

"Hey, where are you going? I don't have to be back until the second trumpet blast." Val looked surprised.

"I have to get back before I'm missed. They might be taking scroll call after the wolf alert." Rapunzel ran out of the barn with a quick wave and a smile.

"What alert? What wolf?" Val called after her.

Rapunzel didn't stay to explain. She'd tell him later. Maybe she'd tell him about her new friends later, too.

Thinking about the girls she'd find at the far courtyard, Rapunzel smiled. And as she jumped the wall of the rose garden and hurried up the stone steps to Princess School, Rapunzel felt completely free.

Chapter Eleven

Best-laid Plans

The mood at Princess School was charged. Although the royal guards had declared the school grounds safe and Ella had tried to tell some of the Bloomers that the wolf wasn't really a wolf, everyone was on edge.

The girl who had been chased by the "wolf" had gone home to her grandmother's house. The rest of the Bloomers were so scared that they walked the hallways in groups or pairs, always looking over their shoulders. Ella walked alone, deep in thought.

Aside from the fact that she was used to being harassed, Ella was simply too exhausted to be afraid. She had been staying up later and later every night. After all of the extra chores were done she had important work of her own to attend to.

Ella had been cleaning the parlor when she came up with the idea. *If only my fairy godmother wasn't so far away*, Ella had thought lamentingly. *Her magic could take care of everything!* Running the feather duster over the scrolled backs of the velvet chairs, she remembered how much fabric had been left over after her stepmother had ordered the seats reupholstered. Kastrid had redecorated everything in the house the moment she moved in. Ella knew the changes had cost her father a small fortune. Kastrid adored spending her new husband's money. But Ella was sure her stepmother had done the redecorating for another reason: to destroy every whisper of her mother's memory. Although her stepmother might be able to make her family's riches disappear, she could not take away Ella's memories. They were safely locked in her head and heart forever.

Ella remembered her mother every day. Her mother had taught her so much before she died, like how to cook and sing, how to dance and garden, how to take care of herself and hold onto hope. Her mother was also the reason Ella could sew better than almost anyone in Stitchery. And there were yards and yards of unused velvet just sitting in the attic.

From the first night Ella had started on her gown she'd stayed up late, working by candlelight to keep her project a secret and to get it finished in time. She'd used one of her mother's too-tattered-to-wear gowns as a basis for the pattern. The gown was simple but elegant. The square neckline was high. The long sleeves were snug but not too tight. And the skirt was full, with tiny pleats going all the way around the bodice. After five nights of hard work, the gown was nearly done.

Maybe it was because she was so tired, but as she moved down the hall Ella felt as if she were in a dream. She could barely believe she would actually be going to the Royal Coronation Ball. She knew her father must have said something because just last night Kastrid had informed her through pursed lips that she could go. Ella supposed Kastrid had gone along with it because she knew her stepdaughter had nothing to wear.

"As long as you are keeping up in school," her stepmother had said tightly, "I can't stop you."

Now all Ella needed was to make it through her classes. But that was a little harder than it sounded. Being tired from her housework and her late-night sewing made it difficult to concentrate. During History: Princesses Past and Present, the letters on her scroll swam in front of her eyes. And when Madame Istoria asked her even a simple question, she sat there, speechless, until Rose whispered the answer in her ear. In Stitchery she kept losing her thread. In Looking Glass she barely had the strength to raise her arms over her head and form a braid! But she would do it. Nothing would keep her from going to the ball now.

Lost in a daze of exhaustion and dreaming of the ball, Ella stumbled in her paper-stuffed glass shoes toward Self-defense. She never even saw Prunilla coming.

"Cin-der-el-la," Prunilla said, drawing out Ella's full name. "Just the Bloomer I've been looking for!"

"Leave me alone, Prunilla. I don't want to be late for class." Ella moved to walk around her stepsister, but Prune quickly stepped back into her path.

"I wouldn't want that, sister dear," Prunilla said with mock sympathy. "It's just that you are so good at cleaning up messes — and I'm afraid there's a rather large one waiting for you in my trunk. I'm sure it won't take you too long to clean out — you already have the rags for the job. Or is that your dress?"

Ella sighed and looked Prunilla in the eye. The "rag" she was talking about used to be Prunilla's. "You might be able to force me to do things in front of your mother, but at school things are different," Ella said.

"Are they really?" Prune asked. The false sweetness was gone, and Prunilla's narrowed eyes looked smaller than ever.

Ella took a small step back. She knew she had just made a big mistake. "Yes," Ella said, her voice cracking.

"Hungh," Prunilla snorted, amused by her own deviousness as she plotted her next cruel act. "We'll just see about that," she growled. "Because if my trunk

isn't organized and scrubbed spotless by the time I am out of Fancy Dress class, I am going to tell Mother that it was *you* who ripped her black fur cape."

Ella's mouth dropped open. She wasn't sure what would be worse — getting in trouble at school or at home. And now it was sure to be both.

Prunilla wasn't even finished. "And if you want to be sure Mother's cape is the only thing that gets ripped, you'll scrub out Hagatha's trunk, too!" With one last nasty glare, Prunilla stomped down the corridor.

When the trumpets blew and classes started, Ella was walking away from the Self-defense classroom door. Almost every shred of hope drained out of her poor tired body as she hurried down the hall toward the older girls' trunks.

She knew she had to take Prunilla's threats seriously. She only hoped that if she did what she was told, her stepsister wouldn't carry out her threats anyway, for spite. All Ella could do was scrub out the trunks as quickly as possible and hope that Madame Lightfoot was more merciful than her stepmother. Ella crossed her fingers. If she wasn't, the little bit of hope she was clinging to would be dashed as well. Trouble in school would be the only excuse Kastrid needed to keep Ella from the Coronation Ball.

Ella lifted the curved lid of Prunilla's trunk and

winced. It was crammed with so much stuff she couldn't even see the velvet lining on the bottom.

It's worse than her closet, Ella thought as a waft of stale air drifted past her nose. With a heavy sigh, Ella began to pull things out — books, scrolls, capes, scarves, scraps of food. . . .

"Need some help?" a voice called out behind her.

Startled, Ella turned around to see Rapunzel, Snow, and Rose.

Ella's eyes widened. "What are you doing here? You're late for class. You'll get in trouble!"

"Correction," Rapunzel said. "We've already been to class. We noticed you weren't there and thought maybe something was wrong. So Rose here faked an injury in Self-defense. We're supposed to be on our way to the nurse's chamber."

"It's strange, but my leg is feeling much better," Rose said with a little smile.

"We still have to go to the nurse, but we have a few minutes to help," Rapunzel said. She surveyed the mess on the corridor floor. "What are you doing, anyway? And what's that smell?"

"That smell is odeur de Prunilla," Ella said. "She's making me clean out her trunk. And Hagatha's, too." Ella felt her throat tighten. "If I don't do it, she's going to get me in trouble with my stepmother!"

"I can't believe those awful girls are part of your family," Rapunzel said. "Maybe living alone in a tower isn't so bad after all," she added thoughtfully.

Snow White was carefully studying Prunilla's trunk. "This isn't as bad as the dwarves' cottage the first time I saw it," she said cheerfully. "If we work together, we can get it cleaned up in no time!"

"Which trunk is Hagatha's?" Rose asked. "Snow and I can clean that one while you and Rapunzel take care of this mess. If we hurry we can get it done and still get to the nurse's chamber before the end of class."

"Thank you!" Ella said, her heart lightening. She pointed to Hagatha's trunk, and the girls got to work organizing books and scrolls into neat piles, folding capes, and throwing out aging food.

"What a waste!" Snow exclaimed, holding up a rotten apple she'd unearthed. "Who lets a perfectly good apple go bad?" Her dark eyes were wide.

"A bad apple like Hagatha," Rapunzel replied grimly as she set a *Riddles and Names* textbook on top of the pile she was making.

They were almost done when Rose pulled a burlap sack out of the bottom of Hagatha's trunk. The sack had a small hole in the bottom, and black fur was sticking out.

"Hey, look at this!" Rose said excitedly. She reached

inside and pulled out a black fur cape with pointed fur triangles, like ears, attached near the collar.

"Wait a second," Rapunzel said. "That looks like a wolf costume!"

"The wolf costume one of my stepsisters was wearing when we were in Frog ID," Ella added.

"It's evidence!" Rapunzel said excitedly. "Now we can figure out a way to get even!"

Just then the five-minute horn blasted — class was almost over!

"We'll have to figure out what to do later," Rose said, quickly shoving the cape back into the bag and the bag back into the compartment. "Let's think about it tonight. Tomorrow we'll come up with a plan."

"You should get to the nurse's chamber," Ella said. "I can finish up here."

"Are you sure?" Snow asked.

"Positive," said Ella. "But you have to hurry or you'll be late!"

Chapter Twelve
Castle Skip-trip

The next morning in hearthroom, Rose watched the door like a hawk. She had a great vantage point from her seat, which was on the opposite side of the chamber from the door. She couldn't wait to see her friends and decide what to do about the fur cape they'd found in Hagatha's trunk. She was sure that Hagatha and Prunilla were responsible for a lot of the tormenting — and now the wolf! Seeking revenge on those nasty girls was going to be sweet!

"How are you going to do your hair for the ball, Beauty?" the girl sitting behind her asked.

Rose was so busy staring at the door she didn't answer. "Rose?" the girl tried again.

"I beg your pardon?" Rose tried not to look annoyed as she turned back to the girl. She didn't care about her hair or the ball! At least not at the moment.

Finally Rapunzel came through the door. But instead of coming right over to Rose, she sat down in her chair and began writing furiously on a scroll. *She must be working on something good,* thought Rose.

Snow came in next. She smiled and waved at Rose — and everyone else in the chamber — before she took her seat near the door. Rose was getting to her feet to go talk to her when Ella shuffled into the room like a scolded puppy. She didn't look at anyone as she took her seat in the back of the chamber.

I guess our plan can wait, Rose thought, sitting back in her chair. Suddenly she was much more worried about something else: Ella. Even though Ella's head was bent low, Rose could see the dark circles under her eyes.

Rose felt a pang of guilt. Here she was always complaining about her overprotective parents and the fawning teachers and princesses. She bet that nobody ever fawned over poor Ella. Those nasty stepsisters of hers made her life miserable — and not only at school, but at home, too! She was sure Ella's stepmother didn't adore Ella the way Rose's parents adored her.

I should count my blessings, Rose thought, *and quit feeling sorry for myself.*

Rose wanted to leap out of her chair and go over to Ella right that minute. But before she could move, Madame Garabaldi strode into the room and began to take scroll call. And then the door opened again, and a page scampered nervously up to Madame G. and handed her a roll of paper.

Rose watched Ella sink lower into her chair. A scroll delivered in hearthroom usually meant that someone was in trouble. And since Ella had missed all of Self-defense yesterday . . . well, it didn't look good.

Ella sat as still as a stone while Madame Garabaldi read the notice. When the teacher looked up, her dark eyes were narrowed over her spectacles at Ella. It took her exactly three seconds to cross to the back of the chamber.

"Cinderella Brown," she said, towering over Ella's small, slouched frame. "I have just been informed that you did not see fit to attend Self-defense class yesterday. Would you like to tell me what pressing engagement you chose to grace with your presence instead?"

Ella looked up at Madame Garabaldi, her face full of desperation. But she said nothing.

"Excuse me?" Madame Garabaldi's eyes dared the cowering girl to speak. "I can't hear you."

Across the chamber, Rapunzel opened her mouth to say something. But after a moment she closed it again. Rose couldn't blame her. Aggravating Madame Garabaldi further wouldn't do anyone any good.

"I see," said Madame Garabaldi, rising to her full height. "Perhaps a punishment of double tower detention would demonstrate to you and the rest of the students that attendance in class is *mandatory* at Princess School." She folded her arms across her chest and glared down at Ella, who was by now halfway under her writing desk.

"Sit up straight!" Madame Garabaldi barked. "Cowering is not acceptable for any princess — even one who has been caught blatantly disregarding the rules."

Rose wanted to leap to her feet and tell Madame Garabaldi to stop being cruel. Detention was punishment enough — especially for Ella, who would also get a second punishment at home. It was excessive to ridicule her in front of the class, too.

Madame Garabaldi turned on her heel, strode back to the front of the chamber, and continued taking scroll call. All eyes were on Ella. Rose tried to get her friend's attention but guessed that a sympathetic smile would not be enough to cheer Ella up. Ella appeared to be using all her strength to hold back tears. She sat staring straight ahead for the rest of class.

Finally, when the end-of-class trumpets sounded, Ella broke down sobbing and raced out of the chamber.

Rose was on her feet in an instant, but still wasn't fast enough. By the time she got out the classroom door Ella was a blur streaking down the corridor. Snow was right behind her. Rose lifted her skirts and hurried ahead, hoping she could catch them.

Just then Hagatha appeared out of nowhere, skipping down the hallway after Snow.

"I'm Snow White," Hagatha called. "I spend all day with dwarves and woodland animals, skipping through the forest!"

Rose saw Ella turn, her eyes full of tears and fury. Ella had clearly reached her breaking point.

Don't do anything, Ella! Rose thought desperately. *You'll just get yourself into more trouble!*

Rose rushed forward to stop her friend. But suddenly there was a swarm of princesses between her and Ella.

"I heard you got hurt in Self-defense," one of them said to Rose. "Are you all right?"

"I'm fine," Rose said brusquely, trying to get through. "I'm trying to get to my friends —"

Out of the corner of her eye, Rose saw Rapunzel break through the throng of princesses. With her left arm, she gently took Snow by the elbow, then did a graceful skip-trip with her right foot, sending Hagatha sprawling to the floor.

"Hey!" Hagatha screeched as Rapunzel linked her free arm through Ella's.

"Come on, girls," Rapunzel said loudly. "Let's go find some decent company."

Rose pushed her way past a final pair of princesses in time to see Ella, Rapunzel, and Snow disappear through the Princess School doors, their arms linked together.

"Help me up!" Hagatha screeched from the floor.

Rose barely heard her. She was too busy watching her new friends go off without her, leaving her alone in a crowd. Again.

Chapter Thirteen
Needle and Hay

"Do you think she is all right?" Snow asked, turning to look back at the fallen Hagatha. "That stone floor is pretty hard."

"Who cares?" Rapunzel replied with a snort. "She was making fun of you, Snow. She was being mean."

Rapunzel pulled Snow and Ella ahead, steering them out the Princess School doors, down the steps, and through the rose garden.

"Don't you know when someone isn't being nice?" Ella asked more gently.

"Not being nice?" Snow repeated aloud. "Why wouldn't a princess be nice? Everyone should be nice, right?" Since she had escaped living with her stepmother, Snow had not encountered anyone who wasn't nice. Not until she came to Princess School, at least.

"Besides, Hagatha's too mean to get hurt," Ella added, striding over the grass.

Snow nodded but now felt even more confused.

Since when did being mean keep someone from getting hurt? If that was true, her stepmother must never feel *any* pain!

"Really? Does being mean keep you from getting hurt?" Snow asked.

"Well, not exactly," Ella admitted.

Snow pushed all thoughts about meanness from her mind. She wanted to savor this moment. She hadn't even been at Princess School for two weeks, and she was out in the gardens with two new friends!

"Come on," Rapunzel said, steering them toward a cozy-looking building with a grass roof. "I want to show you someplace special before class starts."

Snow gasped again. It looked like Rapunzel was leading them toward the stables! She'd been dying to see inside the stables since she'd started at Princess School, to see where the animals lived. And now she was going to!

Rapunzel pushed open one of the heavy stable doors and pulled the girls inside. Holding a finger to her lips, she stood quietly for a minute to make sure the coast was clear. The only audible sounds were of horses munching hay.

"It's safe," Rapunzel reported. "There's nobody else here."

Snow took a deep breath, taking in the smell of clean hay and horses. "Ooooh," she said, excited. The stables were enormous, with row upon row of wooden stalls painted various pastel hues. A well-organized, cream-colored tack room stood just inside the door, housing gleaming saddles and bridles and halters. A giant hayloft extended over half of the ground floor.

"Look at the beautiful horses!" Snow rushed into a lavender stall that was home to a tall chestnut mare. "Hello, sweetie," she greeted, stroking the bridge of the mare's velvety nose. She gazed into the mare's liquid-brown eyes. No matter how much time she spent with them, Snow was always amazed at the gentleness she saw in animals' eyes.

"If I'd known I was coming today, I would have brought you a carrot," she said softly.

The mare let out a soft whinny, nuzzling Snow's arm.

"Next time." Snow giggled. "I promise." She turned in the direction of her friends. "I could stay here all day!" she called.

"Me too," Rapunzel agreed. "But we don't have all day. Come on!"

"Coming!" Snow called back. She wanted to greet each and every horse but knew she couldn't. So she said a quick hello to a few more, promising she'd bring them treats the next time she came, as she made her way back to her friends.

"I'm so sorry about your detention," Rapunzel was

saying. "And Madame Garabaldi. She was being really severe, even for her."

"Maybe she never gets hurt," Snow suggested, plopping down beside Ella.

Ella's eyes glistened with approaching tears. "I think she has it in for me, just like my rotten steps," she said mournfully.

Snow gave Ella's arm a comforting squeeze. "I know what that's like," she said. "My stepmother was so jealous of me, I had to leave my father's castle!"

Ella sighed. "Sometimes I wish I could leave," she said. "But then of course I'd never see my father."

Suddenly Snow felt a little bit sad inside. She knew *exactly* how Ella felt.

"That Hagatha deserves more than to fall flat on her face," Rapunzel announced, changing the subject. She was lying down on the clean straw, gazing up at the stable rafters.

"Tell me about it," Ella agreed, breaking a piece of straw between her fingers. "And what you just saw was her *good* side. She's even more horrible at home."

Snow felt awful for Ella. After all, Ella was just about the nicest person she'd met at Princess School. She reached out a hand to her friend. "Maybe you could come live with the dwarves and me in the forest cottage," she offered.

Ella's eyes welled up with fresh tears at Snow's kindness.

"We've got to do something about Hag," Rapunzel declared, jumping up and pacing the narrow stall. "And her awful sister, too." There was a moment of silence. "Not you, Ella," she added quickly. "Prunilla."

Ella wiped her tears and smiled. "I know," she said. "And *I know*. We *do* have to do something about them. But what?"

The girls were silent for a minute, thinking. And then, in the distance, they heard the muted trumpets signaling the next class.

"Oh my gosh!" Snow said, leaping to her feet.

Ella was up, too. "I can't be late again!" she exclaimed. "They'll lock me up!"

Falling over the skirts of one another's gowns, the girls burst out of the stall. They raced through the stable doors, across the rose garden, and up the Princess School steps.

Throwing open the front door, the girls burst into the school and ran — *smack!* — into Briar Rose.

Rose stood alone in the main entrance, sucking her finger. Her eyes looked a little droopy.

"Oh, no, are you hurt?" Snow asked, pulling Rose's finger from her mouth to take a look.

"It's nothing," Rose yawned. "Just a tiny pinprick. I'll be fine. Please don't fuss."

"What happened?" Ella asked. "You look kind of strange."

"I don't know, really. I just reached into my Stitchery basket and something jabbed my finger." Rose paused to yawn again and rub one of her eyes. "It was a needle, I think. But the funny thing is, I never leave my needles out. I always put them into my metal box."

Ella, Snow, and Rapunzel all looked at one another.

"Are you thinking what I'm thinking?" Ella asked.

"Prunilla was awfully angry when Rose didn't want to go off with her the other day," Snow said, remembering the scowl on the older girl's face.

"Exactly. And Hag and Prune never miss a chance to get even," Ella confirmed.

"Let's go back to the stables and figure out what to do." Rapunzel already had one foot out the door.

"We can't," Ella said. "If we miss class, we'll all get in trouble — Madame Garabaldi might even expel me. And believe me, there's nothing Hagatha and Prunilla would like better."

Chapter Fourteen
Sleeping Beauty

As her friends hurried her down the corridor to Stitchery, Rose's limbs felt weighted down. Her whole body was exhausted.

This is so weird, she thought. *I feel so sleepy.*

She longed to lie right down on the marble floor and take a nap but forced herself to stay awake. *I have to act perfectly normal,* she told herself firmly. *Or my parents are going to go crazy. And the fairies! They'll swarm the castle if they think there's something wrong with me. They might even pull me out of Princess School . . . just when it's getting interesting!*

"Rose, are you okay?" Ella's voice sounded kind of far away, even though Rose was standing right next to her. Rose felt a hand reach out to steady her.

"I'm fine," she said. "I'm just trying to think of what I'm going to tell Madame Taffeta when we get to class." Rose stifled a yawn. "She'll believe anything I say, so I think I should do the talking."

"Fine with me," Rapunzel said as they reached the door to the Stitchery classroom. She looked intently at Rose. "But are you sure you're okay?"

"Perfect," Rose said, trying to sound convincing. Gathering all her strength, she stood up straight and put her hand on the door. She took a deep breath and pushed the door open, leading her friends inside.

Even in her sleepy state, Rose could tell that Madame Taffeta was furious. Or was that panic? Her usually pleasant, round face was tight and her gray eyes looked as sharp as daggers.

"Where have you been?" the teacher asked in a raised voice. "I was so worried I was about to send a message to Madame Garabaldi."

Rose heard Ella gasp and immediately rushed forward, trying not to stumble. She curtsied. "My sincere apologies, Madame Taffeta," she said in her proper princess voice. "I truly regret that I've made all these girls late. You see, I've pricked my finger." She raised her wounded appendage to show the teacher and hide a yawn.

Madame Taffeta gasped in horror as several girls looked over at Rose in concern. "Why, Rose, whatever happened?"

"I came to class early to begin my work," Rose said, feeling almost lucid for the first time since the pinprick. "But while I was threading my needle I accidentally

95

pricked my finger. I hurried to the little princesses' room to rinse it in clean water, and Rapunzel, Ella, and Snow were kind enough to help me and make sure I got safely back to class."

Madame Taffeta inspected the pinprick carefully, making sure it was not too deep. She looked really worried, and Rose felt a little sorry for her. It couldn't be easy to have Madame Garabaldi looking over your shoulder all the time. She probably waited for the teachers to make mistakes just like she did the students!

"Well, it does appear to be just a pinprick," Madame Taffeta said more calmly. "And you girls did a fine job cleaning the wound." She looked at each of the four of them in turn.

"Under the circumstances, I will dismiss your tardiness. I see no reason to report this little incident to Madame Garabaldi."

Rose saw Ella's shoulders relax in relief. She flashed a drowsy smile at her friends. Being the favorite pupil was finally doing some good! But as relief washed over her, so did another wave of sleepiness. All of a sudden she didn't have the strength to fight it anymore. Every pink stone on the cold hard floor looked as inviting as a feather-stuffed pillow. Her eyelids felt incredibly heavy. She needed a nap.

"I think I'll just lie down for a minute," Rose mumbled. Her limbs felt wobbly, like custard. She was grateful for the supportive arms of Rapunzel, Snow, and Ella as they led her over to a pile of large velvet cushions. She had a sleepy memory of having been worried that these girls weren't really her friends. Now she felt sure that they were.

"Is she all right?" Madame Taffeta's voice sounded as if it came from the other end of a long hallway.

"Of course," Rose heard Rapunzel say smoothly. Rose was grateful for her friend's resolve. Rapunzel always managed to stay calm, no matter what the circumstances. "She's just worn out from all the excitement," Rapunzel explained. Rose smiled sleepily. She wasn't sure about any excitement, but she was definitely worn out.

"Beauty is clearly distraught from her episode," Madame Taffeta said, clapping her hands briskly. It sounded to Rose as if Madame Taffeta were now a hundred miles away, but she didn't care. All she cared about was finally being able to sleep. . . .

A dozen pages responded to Madame Taffeta's clap. Scampering into the chamber, they quickly pulled a tapestry from the wall. Six of them held the sides, creating a curving bed, while the others filled it with cushions and helped Rose lie down upon it.

Rose was drifting off contentedly as Madame Taffeta sent another page scurrying to get some blankets. "Hurry now!" she called. "This princess needs a rest!"

Chapter Fifteen

The Perfect Dress

The candelabra beside Ella flickered and she inched closer to it. She could see fairly well in the dim light — she was used to the dark room. But she hoped that the little flames would help warm her cold fingers as she quickly stitched the hem of her ball gown.

Despite the cold and dark, Ella felt unusually happy. There had been no scroll sent home alerting her stepmother of her double tower detention — which hadn't been so terrible after all. She'd used the time to do her homework, and was almost caught up! And since Kastrid had been napping in the afternoons lately, she didn't even realize Ella had gotten home late. Rose had skillfully gotten them off the hook in Stitchery, and — most unbelievable of all — Hagatha and Prunilla hadn't breathed a word of her school trouble for two nights in a row. All her stepsisters talked about was the ball and their beautifully decorated ballot box.

Maybe they don't know about the detention, Ella thought, though it seemed unlikely. It was more probable that they knew that *she* knew about their wolf caper. Knowing Hag and Prune, they were keeping Ella's little secret for now, planning to blackmail her later if she opened her mouth.

It didn't matter. Ella felt too cheerful to let even Hagatha and Prunilla's schemes ruin her mood. With a smile on her face, Ella finished the last stitch on her hem, tied off the thread, and cut it with her teeth. She hung the deep-blue gown before the window and shook out the luxurious fabric of the skirt. With the stars twinkling behind it, the midnight-blue gown looked absolutely magical. It was perfect.

Gazing at the finished dress, Ella felt a little bit like she thought Snow must feel all the time. Without even thinking, she clapped her hands together and began to hum a little tune. It felt good, and before she knew it she was dancing around her tiny room, imagining the fun she was going to have at the ball. She had a dress, she had shoes (so what if they were stuffed with paper and made her a tad clumsy? They were still magic. . . .), and she had new friends. It was too good to be true.

WHAM! Ella's door suddenly burst open, slamming against the stone wall. Hagatha stood in the doorway, panting from the climb up the stairs and holding a torn

99

petticoat — for Ella to mend, no doubt. Her beady eyes grew round when she saw Ella dancing.

Ella quickly tried to appear unhappy. Wiping the smile off her face, she slumped down beside the mending pile with a heavy sigh. Hagatha would take extra delight in tormenting her if she realized she was in a great mood.

"What's going on in here?" Hagatha puffed into the room holding the torn petticoat. "I was just bringing up this mending and I thought I heard singing." Hagatha looked around like she expected to find a chamber choir in the corner.

"Must have been the wind," Ella said, staring down at her lap and trying to look miserable. "My window doesn't shut all the way" — she gestured toward the window — "and sometimes . . ."

Ella trailed off. She followed Hagatha's gaze to the dress that hung from the windowsill and gasped.

She had made a terrible mistake. All she could do was hold her breath and wait to see what Hag would do next.

"It's perfect," Hagatha breathed. She rubbed her hands together as if to warm them before reaching out to touch the beautiful velvet fabric.

Ella cringed. "I, uh, made it myself," she explained. It sounded as if Hagatha's compliment had been almost genuine.

"It'll look *gorgeous* at the ball." Hagatha pulled the skirts across her chest. "On me. Doesn't it go well with my eyes? In this dress I will be crowned for sure!"

If she weren't completely horrified, Ella would have laughed out loud. The beautiful blue of the gown *might* match Hagatha's eyes, but they were so small and beady, no one would ever be able to tell. And the thought of anyone voting for Hagatha . . . it was too much.

"You won't be wearing that dress," Ella said, standing and mustering up as much courage as she could. "I will. I made it for myself." Ella swept the dress off the hanger and clutched it to her chest.

"You?" Hagatha scoffed. "You aren't even going to the ball!"

"I am so," Ella argued. "Father said so. Your mother agreed!"

Hagatha smiled slowly. She seemed more and more like Kastrid all the time. "That was before I told her about your trouble in school, Cinder dear."

"You didn't." Ella dropped onto her hard wood-frame bed.

"Of course I did." Hagatha held a hand out for the dress. "I didn't want you there embarrassing us. And don't worry, Mother will think of a suitable punishment so you don't miss class again." Hagatha jiggled her hand impatiently, waiting for Ella to give her the dress.

101

"Maybe I can't wear this dress, but neither will you," Ella said, standing up and moving to the far side of her small room. "I could tell your mother a few things, you know — like the things we found in your trunk!"

"I'll say you're lying," Hagatha shouted.

"My friends were with me," Ella yelled back.

"I'll tell her you planted it, then!" Hagatha was seething. She stomped her feet. Her face was red and blotchy and she was stepping closer and closer to Ella with each second.

"Girls!"

Without warning, a tall figure appeared in the door and Hagatha and Ella both fell silent. Kastrid appeared so suddenly, Ella was not sure how much she had heard. Or what she was going to say. With one step, Kastrid seemed to fill Ella's small room entirely. Behind her, Prunilla poked her head in, obviously not wanting to miss the fun.

"You *know* I cannot abide bickering," Kastrid said softly with her eyes closed. Then, without warning, she erupted like a volcano. "SO TELL ME WHAT IS GOING ON!"

"Mummy, she won't let me wear that dress," Hagatha whined and pointed at the dress Ella was still holding before wiping her nose on her sleeve.

"Of course she will," Kastrid said, her voice returning to a syrupy smoothness. She held out a long slen-

102

der hand to Ella, who had no choice but to lay the gown across it. Though Ella had threatened to tell on Hagatha for all of the mean tricks, deep down she knew it was useless. Kastrid would believe whatever she wanted to, and that would be her daughters' lies. Even Ella's father was helpless when it came to dealing with Kastrid. When Kastrid was around, everything always went the way Hagatha and Prunilla wanted.

Kastrid held the dress up, inspecting it. She ran the material between her fingers and a small smile played on her lips.

"It's m-mine," Ella stammered foolishly. "I made it."

Kastrid turned. "With whose material?" she asked slowly, looking Ella right in the eye.

Ella was caught. In a moment her stepmother would be accusing her of stealing. Not that Kastrid would ever have used the remnants — until now they had been mere scraps to her. But the fabric wasn't really Ella's. Ella hung her head and braced herself for the lecture.

She did not expect the one she got.

"It doesn't matter." Kastrid held the gown up to Hagatha, and Prunilla rushed into the room for a closer look. "It doesn't matter because, Cinderella, you will not be going to the ball."

"But you said —" Ella protested, though she knew it was hopeless.

"I said you might go if you were doing well in school. Which your sisters tell me you are not." Kastrid looked at Ella disapprovingly. "I wish I could say I am surprised. I only hope your father can bear the shame should you be expelled."

Ella's face was hot. How dare Kastrid mention her father? He would never be ashamed of her! She would never be expelled from Princess School. Why, with the trouble Hagatha and Prunilla caused, *they* should be the ones to get expelled.

Ella longed to scream back at her stepmother. She wanted to yell at her: *You should be ashamed. Look at your daughters. They are such awful witches, they belong in the Grimm School!*

"The dress won't fit Hagatha," was all Ella could mumble. Her stepsister was much taller and heavier than Ella.

"Well, then, you will have to *make* it fit." Kastrid threw the dress on the bed beside Ella. "In time for the Coronation Ball, of course."

With that, Ella's stepmother turned and swept out of the room and down the long flight of stairs.

Prunilla looked as if she was about to roll on the floor laughing. Hagatha was grinning, too. "And I'll need this petticoat," she said, tossing down the torn garment in her best imitation of her mother. "By tomorrow." Then she turned and followed her sister out of the room.

Ella collapsed across her bed. And though Hagatha had slammed the door behind her, Ella could still hear her stepsisters' wicked cackling over her own quiet sobs.

Chapter Sixteen
Wake-up Call

"Maybe I should transfer to *your* school," Val said. He sounded serious. "Nothing that exciting is going on over at Charm — it's all codes and chivalry."

"That's not even half of it," Rapunzel said, picking up a flat rock as they passed the mill pond. "We think maybe Ella's horrid stepsisters are behind the drenchings and the pea incident in addition to the wolf stunt. You would not *believe* these girls. They're like miniature Madame Gothels!"

Rapunzel sent the rock sailing over the still water. It skipped once, twice, three times before sinking to the bottom of the pond. She was enjoying bragging to Val. Princess School really was exciting. "I think they might have been the ones to stash that needle in Rose's bag, too. Luckily she wasn't hurt too badly."

Val flung the rock he was holding and didn't even watch to see how many times it skipped. "Beauty's been hurt?" he asked. His voice was full of concern, and he grabbed Rapunzel's arm. "What happened? Is she okay?"

"She's fine." Rapunzel shook Val off her arm. "Just tired is all." She looked at Val with narrowed eyes. "Is this part of the whole chivalry thing? What's the big deal? She just pricked her finger!"

Rapunzel picked up her books and walked away from Val, down the road toward their schools. She was annoyed. Sometimes Val was a little *too* interested in Rose. Her every move seemed to fascinate him. But maybe there was reason to be concerned. Rose had been awfully hard to wake up after Stitchery. And yesterday she had almost fallen asleep again in every class. For two days her head had been bobbing around on her neck like a sprung jack-in-the-box — hardly a pretty sight.

"Wait up." Val jogged beside her. "Don't be jealous."

"Ha!" Rapunzel laughed. Jealous of what? Rose was even more of a prisoner than she was. It was astounding the way her family doted on her. They were always waiting for her the moment school ended and accompanying her in the morning, trying to get her to wear ridiculous protective clothing. Rose even told her that she thought the fairies spied on her during the day. If you asked Rapunzel, that much attention would be worse than being locked in a tower alone. Everyone was always so worried about Rose.

Rapunzel started walking again, fast. Then she broke into a run.

"Hey," Val called after her. "Hey!"

Rapunzel waved but did not slow her pace. She wanted to get to school early. She had some things to discuss with Ella, Snow, and Rose.

Rapunzel scanned the crowd on the bridge as she rushed across the moat. There was Snow. Snow spotted Rapunzel, too, and skipped over with a wave and a warm smile. Rapunzel raised her head and gave a nod, but she didn't smile. She was too worried. What if Rose had gotten worse after school yesterday?

With a crushing wave of relief, Rapunzel spotted Rose on the other side of the bridge. She was holding a large mug of tea and brushing off her fairies and parents. She still looked tired but very much alive. Rose saw Snow and Rapunzel, too, and started to make her way over.

As Rapunzel watched Rose try to shake her fairies and join them on the steps, she couldn't really blame Val for liking the girl. In addition to being beautiful, she was great. And so were her other new friends, Snow and Ella.

Speaking of which, where *was* Ella? Beyond the bridge on the muddy lane, Rapunzel saw a forlorn figure walking slowly toward the school. The girl's skirts dragged in the mud and her head hung so low it was surprising it wasn't getting wet and muddy, too. Ella.

Without a word, Rapunzel headed for her crestfallen friend. Snow followed. But Rose, who had waved her parents off at last, slumped against the chain of the drawbridge. She yawned as Snow and Rapunzel whisked past. "I just have to rest a moment," she said sleepily. "I'll catch up."

Ella looked worse close up than she did from a distance. Her eyes were red from crying. Her hair was a mess, even by Rapunzel's standards. And her shoulders were so slumped she looked like she was carrying the whole world upon them.

Poor thing, Rapunzel thought as she hurried to Ella's side. *She has to go home to Hag and Prune every night. And her stepmother!*

Ella stumbled in her paper-stuffed shoes and almost fell into the carriage ruts. Rapunzel and Snow got there just in time, and Ella leaned heavily on her friends' shoulders.

"I can't go to the ball," she sobbed. "Hagatha . . . told. . . . She . . ." Ella was crying too hard to even speak. It took several minutes for her to tell the whole story. By the time she finished, Rapunzel was fuming. Even Snow looked angry.

"How could they?" Snow asked, dumbfounded. "Why would they? It's just . . . it's just so *mean*!"

"That's right," Rapunzel said, herding her friends back toward the bridge where Rose was dozing on her feet. "I think somebody needs to teach them to be nicer. Lots nicer."

"That's a great idea!" Snow chirped.

Rapunzel chewed her braid. Ella nodded at her and, in spite of her sad face, Rapunzel could tell by the look in her eyes she was ready to strike back no matter what it cost.

The trumpets blasted a two-minute warning and most of the princesses picked up their skirts and headed inside.

Rapunzel's head was spinning. The ball was only two days away. There was no way she was going to let Ella miss it or her awful stepsisters enjoy it. But they would have to act fast.

"Wake up, Brainy Rose." Rapunzel gently flicked Rose with the end of her braid, startling her awake.

"I'm fine. I'm fine." Rose stood up straight, sloshing the giant mug of tea.

"I'm glad to hear it," Rapunzel said honestly. "Because we need your help." She pulled her friends into a tight circle. "We've got to come up with a plan. And we don't have much time."

Chapter Seventeen
Daring Rescue

Ella peered out of the small open window on the top floor of her father's manor. For once she was glad that Kastrid had moved her room to the distant turret over the kitchen, far from the other bedrooms in the house. There was less of a chance anyone would notice the slim figure climbing her way, stone by stone, up the outside wall. It was so dark, Ella could hardly see Rapunzel herself.

"Are you still there?" Ella whispered into the night.

"Of course," Rapunzel said. Her head appeared just below the window opening and she hitched a leg up over the windowsill. "Could you give me a hand, damsel in distress?"

Ella laughed. "My hero," she said, dragging Rapunzel through the small opening. Rapunzel fell the rest of the way through and onto the knotted rag rug Ella had painstakingly woven from small scraps of cloth.

"Ooph." The heavy sack tied across Rapunzel's

back flattened her to the floor. Ella stared. Even in this inelegant pose, Rapunzel looked regal in a lovely dark green velvet gown with golden ribbons woven through the sleeves.

"No time for swooning, Princess," Rapunzel said as she got to her feet. "We've got work to do if we're going to get you to the ball in time." Rapunzel handed Ella the sack and went back to the window. "Get going. I'll watch for our prince."

Ella could feel her heart pounding in her chest. She had never done anything this risky before. Or this fun.

With the bag slung over her shoulder like laundry, she tiptoed downstairs to her stepsisters' dressing rooms.

In Hagatha's room, Ella's blue ball gown hung at the ready. She had spent hours ripping out stitches and redoing them. And since Hagatha was going to the ball in a newly made gown, Prunilla had announced that Ella would have to refit *her* dress as well, embellishing it with additional ribbons and lace. Ella had taken careful measurements of both her stepsisters. "Mother always said the proper fit is important," she had told them.

"That's right!" Prunilla had snapped back at her. "So don't mess up, dunderhead."

Ella was sure she hadn't messed up. Both dresses would fit like the girls had been sewn into them. They would be . . . breathtaking. Literally. The gowns would be so tight, her stepsisters wouldn't be able to take a deep breath. But Ella knew Hag and Prune would be too vain to admit that their dresses were too small. Instead they would suffer through the evening, puffing and wheezing around the dance floor. Ella almost giggled at her own deviousness. And the gowns were only part of the plan.

Beneath each altered gown, Ella had already laid out each sister's pair of shoes. Now she replaced them with almost identical footwear . . . two sizes smaller.

The shoes had been Rapunzel's idea. But it was Snow who had made it happen. Snow's dwarves were friends with some talented elfin shoemakers who had crafted the replicas in exchange for a few of Snow's delicious pies. Ella ran a finger along the soft leather and giggled. The elves had done a wonderful job.

Ella stooped to retrieve Hag's and Prune's regular shoes but stopped when she felt Rapunzel's sack bump against her leg. There was something else inside. Digging down to the bottom, Ella pulled out a beautiful pair of golden suede shoes with tiny rosettes stitched to the sides. They were just her size. Ella's breath caught. Could they really be for her?

Slipping off one of her oversized glass shoes, Ella slid her small foot into the soft suede. It fit like a glove. She tried on the other and glanced at her reflection in the full-length dressing room mirror. The shoes were truly lovely, and as comfortable as a pair of well-worn slippers.

Ella picked up her stepsisters' properly sized shoes and stuffed them into Rapunzel's bag along with her glass slippers. Then she took one last look in the mirror at the golden beauties on her feet . . . and noticed that the door behind her was opening!

Ella slipped noiselessly out the chambermaid's exit and silently thanked Snow for the shoes. If she'd been wearing her awkward glass slippers she would have been caught for sure.

Upstairs, Rapunzel was walking slowly around Ella's bedroom. "Your room isn't much better than mine," she said when Ella came back in. She smiled down at the sight of the slippers on Ella's feet. "Pretty, aren't they?"

Ella nodded, a smile spreading across her face. "Beautiful," she said.

"Are your sisters getting ready?"

"They were just coming into the dressing room when I left. I almost got caught!" Ella said. She felt nervous and excited at the same time. She and Rapunzel giggled nervously. They could not keep still. Ella was eager to see the results of her handiwork, but she would have to wait.

At last Ella saw a tiny light flare outside. A moment later something shiny caught the light and reflected it into Ella's window. That was the signal.

Hagatha and Prunilla had been sent off in the carriage — the road would be clear.

Rapunzel took a hand mirror out of her pocket and flashed back. Then she unwound her l-o-n-g braid, tying one end around Ella's waist in case she fell. After helping Ella out the window, Rapunzel climbed out slowly behind her.

Ella's stomach flipped when she got all the way outside.

"Just take it easy. Feel the rocks with your toes and fingers and don't move until you've got a good hold." Rapunzel's voice above her was reassuring. "And don't worry — my hair has got you, too!"

"To your left," Val coached from the ground, shining his light up to help the girls.

"Don't listen to him. He can't climb a tree," Rapunzel joked.

"I heard that!" Val protested.

It was easier to climb down the wall than Ella thought. With a final leap she landed on the ground. She felt exhilarated.

"Ella, Val. Val, Ella." Rapunzel gestured between the two while she quickly recoiled her hair.

115

"Charmed," Val took Ella's hand and bowed deeply. His velvet breeches were caramel colored, and the tunic and cape he wore were deep burgundy.

"Likewise," Ella said with a giggle as Val helped her up onto the horse standing nearby. When Ella was seated sidesaddle, the young prince took his seat behind her and held another hand out to Rapunzel.

Rapunzel refused the hand, swinging up behind Val by holding onto the saddle and boosting herself up on a nearby rock. For the first time Ella noticed that Rapunzel's skirts were split like pants, but the slit was cleverly hidden in pleats. Smart.

"Let's ride," Rapunzel said when the three were all safely on the horse. Val flicked the reins. Ella grabbed the horse's mane and without another word they galloped down the dark road toward Princess School and the Royal Coronation Ball.

The towers of Princess School were bathed in flickering torchlight. Gilded flags flew from the castle turrets. And every guard, page, and trumpeter was dressed in purple and gold and standing in a long line that marked the entry to the school. Tonight was going to be a magical night.

As they raced by on horseback, Ella saw princes and princesses arriving in fine coaches. Even the teams of horses were dressed up with plumes on their heads and silver bells on their halters.

Skirting the edges of the school, Val turned his horse and nudged him with his heels. The horse went from a gallop to a run. Before Ella could cry out in alarm, she and the horse and Val and Rapunzel were sailing over the Princess School moat and trotting toward the stables. When they entered the warm stables Ella slid to the hay-strewn floor with a wide smile on her face. Already this had been one of the best nights of her life.

"You made it!" Snow called. She elbowed Rose awake and pulled her out of the stall they had been hiding in. Snow and Rose both looked lovely. Snow's deep-red gown was the color of her ruby lips and looked so elegant against her alabaster skin that it didn't matter that the hem was too short or that the collar was old-fashioned. And Rose! Her gown was lavender satin with tiny opalescent pearls stitched over the bodice and skirt. Ella noticed that Val seemed to think Rose looked beautiful as well — he was staring at her with his mouth slightly open.

"I guess you'd better see to King," Rapunzel said, kicking Val lightly in the shin. "You know, your *horse*?"

Val quickly pulled his eyes away from Rose and closed his mouth. "Of course," he said. "I'll see you ladies at the ball."

117

"Did you get the shoes?" Snow asked.

"Oh, yes!" Ella replied. She lifted her tattered gown to show her friends. "They're beautiful. Thank you so much!"

"Ella, look!" Snow exclaimed. "Rose and I brought you something to wear, too!" Next to the horse bridles hung two ball gowns. Ella knew at once which one was Snow's — the hard white collar was a dead giveaway. Maybe Snow could pull off that look with her pale skin, dark eyes, and red lips, but Ella's delicate features would be lost in the stiff whiteness.

The other dress was from Rose's collection. It was pale, pale blue like the summer sky through a thin layer of cloud, but it shone golden on the edges like sun peeking through.

"You have to wear this one," Rose yawned, sitting down on a bale of hay. "It'll look royal on you."

Rapunzel agreed, and Ella slipped the dress on.

"Oh!" Snow cried as soon as the tiny buttons on the back of Ella's dress had been hooked and she spun around to show the girls. Snow couldn't say anything more. The fit was perfect.

"What about the hair?" Rapunzel raised an eyebrow. Ella noticed for the first time that Rapunzel's auburn tresses looked perfect. Her large braid was actually made up of hundreds of tiny braids woven together and then coiled around the back of her head like a bun. The end of the braid (she could never twist *all* of it into a bun) was tied off with a green ribbon that matched her dress. A few wispy curls framed her face. What had happened to the girl who seemed out of place in Looking Glass class? She had obviously been practicing more than communication signals with that hand mirror of hers!

"I think I have an idea," Rapunzel said, sitting Ella down on a hay bale and reaching for the hairbrush Rose had brought. She twisted and wove Ella's yellow tresses while Rose lazily pinched some color into Ella's cheeks, helped her with her gloves and jewels, and wove a satin ribbon through the bodice of her dress. Ella felt like royalty as her friends bustled around her.

"I think that's it." Rose stepped back, trying to hide another enormous yawn.

Rapunzel loosened a few strands of Ella's hair near her face and smiled at her own handiwork.

Standing up, Ella spun around to face her friends. The dress caught the light of the lanterns burning by the horse stalls. Ella's loosely swept-up hair revealed her happy face. She glowed.

Snow, Rapunzel, and Rose drew in their breath. They could not help but stare.

"What is it? What's the matter? Did I get it dirty?" Ella looked down at the shimmering skirts of her gown. "Do I look awful?"

"No. It's just that . . . it's just that you look so beautiful!" Snow exclaimed. Rose and Rapunzel nodded in agreement.

"Here." Rapunzel pulled the hand mirror back out of her pocket. "See for yourself."

Ella gazed at her reflection in the mirror for a long moment. From the curl on her forehead to the tips of her toes she felt beautiful — not just like a princess — like a queen. Like a queen on her way to a ball!

Ella's wet eyes sparkled as she looked gratefully at her three smiling friends. "Thank you," she said, choking up. She rushed toward them with her arms open for a hug. "I could never have made it here without you!"

Chapter Eighteen
The Ball

Smiling and holding hands, the four girls headed out of the stables and across the gardens to the castle.

"We have to go through the front," Rapunzel said, steering everyone around the low wall that separated the rose garden from the main entrance. "So everyone can see the beautiful princess." She winked at Ella, and all four girls giggled. Ella beamed. She really did feel like royalty.

The girls rounded the end of the wall, and the glorious sight of the illuminated castle overwhelmed Ella once again. The flags hanging from the turrets blew gently in the night breeze. The torchlights flickered, casting gentle shadows on the castle walls. The school was truly an enchanting sight.

Making their way across the bridge, the girls pulled Rose along with them. Ella noticed that she was practically sleepwalking.

"Are you all right, Rose?"

Rose yawned, but opened her eyes wide. "I'm completely fine," she replied blearily.

As the girls lifted their skirts to ascend the castle stairs, several of the pages stopped trumpeting to watch them pass. At first Ella thought they were looking at Rose. But some of them seemed to be staring in her direction.

They couldn't be looking at me, Ella thought shyly as they entered the castle. *Could they?* It was all too dreamy. Ella wondered what Kastrid would think if she saw her now. She smiled wider just thinking about it. For once her stepmother would be speechless.

Inside, the girls made their way to the ballroom. When they stepped through the carved double doors, all four of them stopped to take in the breathtaking sight.

The marble floor had been polished to a sparkling shine. Colorful silk streamers hung from the walls and pillars. At one end, a long banquet table was covered with delicious meats and pastries and punch. At the other, an orchestra played a lively waltz on a small raised stage. Just to the right was the ballot box, gaudily decorated with too many ribbons and bows.

That's Hagatha and Prunilla for you, Ella thought wryly.

"Let's dance!" Snow chirped, pulling the others

toward the dance floor, where several princes and princesses were already whirling about.

"I'd love to" — Rose yawned — "but I need to rest a minute first."

"I'll come with you," Ella offered.

"I can stay with Rose," a voice said from behind them. It was Val. Ella had almost forgotten he was with them.

"Of course you will," Rapunzel said, rolling her eyes.

"That would be wonderful!" Snow exclaimed, linking Rose's arm through Val's. "Come on, girls!"

Rapunzel looked a little irritated, but she let Snow lead her and Ella onto the dance floor. Right away the girls began to sway daintily to the music. Or at least, Ella and Rapunzel did. Snow seemed to have her own kind of dance style, which included a lot of leaping and flapping.

I wonder if the deer and the birds taught her those steps, Ella thought, smiling to herself.

"Nice moves," Rapunzel said slyly.

"Oh, do you like them?" Snow cried, hopping up and down like a rabbit. "The animals and I have been practicing!"

"Well, they're original," Rapunzel said, smiling affectionately at her friend. Ella had to laugh. Snow could be silly, all right. But she was also the sweetest person she'd ever met, and full of surprises.

"Excuse me," came a voice from behind them. "May I have this dance?"

Ella whirled around and found herself staring into the blue eyes of a handsome, dapperly dressed prince.

Ella was so surprised, she didn't say anything at first. Was he talking to her?

Next to her, Snow giggled. The prince held out his hand. "I am Allister," he said. "And I would be most pleased if you would dance with me."

Blushing, Ella nodded and took the boy's hand. As he whisked her away, Ella saw the smiling faces of her friends whoosh by. She felt light-headed, as if she might faint. Only she wouldn't, of course. If she did, she might miss something!

Allister was a wonderful dancer. He made Ella feel light and graceful on her feet as he turned her this way and that. Ella's head was spinning faster than her feet on the dance floor. In the Princess School ballroom, surrounded by her friends, she felt completely at home. Cinderella felt . . . right. She sighed as the music ended. She never wanted to lose this feeling. She happily agreed when Allister asked her to dance again.

Ella and Allister danced three times — until another boy cut in.

"May I have a turn?" he asked smoothly.

Allister nodded, bowed to Ella, and stepped away.

"I am Sebastian," the boy said. He was shorter than

Allister, and Ella guessed that he was in his first year at the Charm School. His dance steps were somewhat stilted and he kept counting to himself, but Ella didn't mind. She was having, well, a ball!

Sebastian only got one dance with Ella before another boy stepped in — and another, then another. Ella was grateful that she was wearing comfortable shoes. Her feet never would have survived all this dancing in glass!

Whirling atop the shining pink marble floor, Ella and her dance partner — a handsome, curly-haired boy named Ian — seemed to be in a private pocket of air. Several of the other dancers had stopped to watch them. They were murmuring and nodding approvingly. Ella couldn't recall ever getting so much attention! Peering around the crowd, Ella half hoped that her stepsisters weren't among the people watching. Hagatha and Prunilla were awful enough to ruin even this moment. But with a mischievous smile Ella changed her mind. She hoped Hag and Prune would see her! They would probably be too shocked to do anything.

Ella was just thinking she might need to take a rest when Rapunzel tapped her on the shoulder.

"Come quick," she whispered, sounding a little frantic. "It's your stepsisters!"

"Excuse me," Ella told her dance partner. "I have to attend to something."

125

His face full of disappointment, the prince nodded and bowed slightly. "Of course," he said.

"Those awful girls are stuffing the ballot box!" Rapunzel reported as she led Ella toward the stage. Sure enough, Hag was standing guard in front of the box. Behind her, Prune was stuffing scroll after scroll into the slot at the top.

"Hurry up!" Hagatha snapped at her sister. "We don't have all night!"

"I've just started. *You* try shoving all these scrolls in here," Prunilla snapped back. "My gown is so tight I can barely lift my arms!"

Ella knew she would get in trouble if her sisters saw her at the ball, but as she stormed forward, she didn't care. She was emboldened by her fancy gown and good friends. No one could tell her she didn't belong at Princess School — certainly not her awful stepsisters. It was time to put a stop to their torment. She would not allow them to rig the vote for Princess of the Ball!

"What do you think you're doing?" she asked, planting herself right in front of Hagatha. She glanced down at the too-tight bodice of her gown and tried not to smile. Her stepsister looked like a sausage!

"You!" Hagatha tried to sneer, but it came out more as a gasp. Her eyes narrowed but quickly widened again as she looked Ella up and down. Even nasty Hagatha could not hide her admiration.

126

"What are you doing here?" Prunilla panted over her sister's shoulder. Her gaze held on the lovely gown Ella wore.

"Attending the ball, of course," Ella said, gazing directly at Prunilla.

"Never mind that," Rapunzel cut in. "What are *you* doing to the ballot box?"

"Ah, yes, the ballot box," Headmistress Bathilde echoed as she approached the girls. The headmistress's stiff silk skirts swished with each step. The people in her path fell silent with awe and drew out of her way. Her willowy frame seemed to float over the ground, making her look taller than she actually was, and her face showed few of her numerous years.

Lady Bathilde cast her silvery eyes on the ballot box. "You must agree it's quite thoroughly decorated," she stated. Beside her, Madame Taffeta watched Hagatha and Prunilla closely.

Ella wasn't sure if the headmistress intended what she said to be a compliment or not, but she thought she saw an unusual sort of smile on Madame Taffeta's face.

"It's time to count the ballots," the headmistress added smoothly.

"Oh, of course," Hagatha said in a sweet but high-pitched voice as she and Prunilla stepped aside.

"We were just guarding it for you," Prunilla peeped.

"To make sure nobody tampered with the voting scrolls." She let out a puff of air and clutched her stomach.

"Yeah, right," Rapunzel said, glaring openly at the older girls.

"Are you all right, Prunilla?" Madame Taffeta asked Prunilla. "You look a bit . . . blue." She seemed to be eyeing the girls' gowns suspiciously, and Ella had a moment of panic.

"We're fine, of course," Prunilla replied. This time her voice almost sounded normal, but she still fidgeted in her golden gown.

"Yes. We were just going to get something to eat," Hagatha rasped.

As Hagatha and Prunilla limped away, Ella tried not to laugh. If either of them ate a single bite, she'd definitely rip a seam!

"Come on," Rapunzel said. "Let's go find Rose and Snow."

Disappointed, Ella nodded and followed her friend away from the ballot box. Part of her wanted to tell the headmistress and Madame Taffeta what Hag and Prune had been up to. But although their actions had looked totally suspicious, they didn't have any actual proof. And besides, why would the headmistress believe a couple of Bloomers? If the teachers didn't trust the older girls, they wouldn't have let them decorate the ballot box to begin with!

As she and Rapunzel crossed the ballroom, Ella struggled with what to do. Then, suddenly, she noticed that people were staring at her.

"What's going on?" she whispered to Rapunzel.

"They're gazing at the belle of the ball," Rapunzel replied with a grin.

Ella thought Rapunzel might be teasing, and whacked her playfully on the arm. But by then they had already reached their friends.

Rose was sitting with Val and Snow on the edge of the dance floor, her drooping head dipping dangerously low to the heaping plate of food she held.

"I'll take that," Rapunzel said, removing the plate before Rose's face fell into the meat pies. "I need to drown my sorrows at our defeat."

"Help yourself," Rose replied sleepily.

"What defeat?" Val asked.

"We think Ella's nasty stepsisters were trying to rig the vote. We caught them stuffing ballots into the box."

"How do you know they weren't real ballots?" Snow asked.

Ella sighed. Sometimes she wished she could be more like Snow — always trusting and expecting the best of people. But living with her stepmother and stepsisters had made that impossible.

"Because we're talking about Hagatha and Prunilla," Rapunzel said.

"Exactly," Ella agreed.

"Excuse me," said a prince as he approached. He stopped directly in front of Ella and stared down at the floor nervously. "Would you like to dance?"

"No thank you," Ella said as kindly as she could. "I'm spending a little time with my friends."

The boy looked crestfallen.

"But I would love to dance later," Ella added.

The boy looked up, grinning from ear to ear. "All right!" he said excitedly as he bounded away.

"I think you've put a spell on everyone here, Ella," Val teased. "Everybody keeps staring at you and whispering."

Ella blushed. "It's Rose's gown, Rapunzel's hairstyling talent, and Snow's shoes," she said modestly.

"Oh, no!" Snow said. "The elves made those shoes for you. They're for you to keep!"

Ella gave Snow a hug. She hardly ever got new items of clothing — and nothing as beautiful as these suede shoes. "Thank you!" she cried.

"And for the record, it's not the gown or the shoes — or your hair," Rapunzel said. "It's *you*, Ella. You're glowing."

"Princes and Princesses," called a loud voice. It was Lady Bathilde. "Please gather around the stage. It is time to crown the Princess of the Ball!"

"Come on!" Snow said excitedly.

Helping Rose to her feet, the girls and Val made their way to the stage. Ella saw Hagatha and Prunilla right up front, still fidgeting with their gowns.

Tapping the school scepter on the stage floor and holding a glittering crown aloft, Lady Bathilde stood with her back straight. Her mere presence demanded attention. The crowd quieted, and she slowly began to unroll an ornate scroll that held the winner's name.

"This year's Princess of the Ball is . . ."

"Move over!" a voice rasped out. Ella recognized it at once. Hagatha.

"That crown is mine," Prunilla hissed back.

There was a scuffle as the two girls tried to grab for the crown, nearly knocking over the headmistress. Then Hagatha tripped on the hem of her gown and fell over, dragging Prunilla down with her.

On the stage, Lady Bathilde was ignoring the scuffle quite successfully. Looking over the waiting crowd, she smiled as she announced the winner's name: Cinderella Brown!

Chapter Nineteen

A True Princess

Ella was so shocked when she heard her name that she didn't move. Beside her, her friends squealed with delight.

"It's you! It's you!" Snow cried, clapping her hands together.

Rose gave her a giant hug. "You deserve it," she said with a yawn.

Rapunzel nudged her forward. "You have to go up to the stage," she said. "Your tiara is waiting."

"No!" Prunilla shrieked. On her hands and knees, she was still trying to grab the tiara out of Lady Bathilde's hands.

"It's mine!" Hagatha screamed.

One of the older Charm School princes near the front unceremoniously pulled the girls to their feet. "It's not yours, or yours," he said firmly, eyeing each girl with disgust. "It's Ella's."

"But she, she —"

"She is the Princess of the Ball," the prince said flatly.

Several of the princesses in the crowd began to laugh at Hagatha and Prunilla, who were so dumb-founded by the prince's words that they were actually speechless. As the laughter grew, the girls slinked toward the ballroom door and their waiting carriage, wheezing and limping the entire way.

As Ella watched them go, she realized she would be in big trouble when she got home. But as she stepped onto the stage she didn't care.

Lady Bathilde smiled majestically as she placed the tiara on Ella's head. Then she put her hands on Ella's shoulders and turned her slowly to face the crowd. The ballroom erupted into claps and cheers. Looking down at her schoolmates and her new friends, Ella felt like a true princess.

When the coronation ceremony was over, even more princes were vying for dances with Ella. But after she danced her promised dance with the boy who had asked her earlier, she kindly declined them all. This was a moment she wanted to share with her friends.

"Do you get to keep it?" Snow asked, fingering the tiara on Ella's head.

"I don't think so," Ella said. "They need it again for next year's ball. But just wearing it is wonderful enough."

Suddenly the music was interrupted a second time

and a regal-looking woman in a black gown and flowing black cape took the stage.

"Who's that?" Rapunzel asked, her eyes wide.

"That's Malodora," Val whispered. "She's the headmistress at the Grimm School. Not someone you want to mess with."

Ella shuddered. Just the sight of this woman was enough to scare anyone. She made Kastrid look friendly! She glanced at her friends to gauge their reactions. Rose looked as sleepy as ever. Rapunzel looked wary. And Snow looked three shades whiter.

"Snow?" Ella put a hand on her friend's arm. "What is it? Are you okay?"

Snow's free hand squeezed the one Ella had placed on her arm, but her eyes never left the stage. "That's my stepmother," she said in a frightened whisper.

Waving her hand through the air dramatically, Malodora made an important announcement.

"The Grimm School and Princess School will be holding the annual Maiden Games exactly one month from today," she said in a booming voice. "Everyone will participate, and I myself, along with Lady Bathilde, will oversee the Games. The winners will receive the coveted Golden Ball."

"Wow," Ella breathed.

"Games!" Rapunzel cried excitedly, hopping up and down. "I love competition!"

Rose slumped even more heavily against Val, finally completely asleep.

"Oh, no," Snow said, her dark eyes wide with fear.

"Don't worry, Snow," Ella said comfortingly. "Whatever it is, we'll help you through it."

"That's right," Rapunzel agreed, coming to her other side.

Snow smiled, but Ella sensed that she was still afraid. Ella couldn't blame her. Malodora was clearly a force to be reckoned with. And she knew all about sinister stepmothers.

"Maybe we should move Rose to a corner and lay her down," Rapunzel suggested.

"Oh, I'm fine," Val replied, but he was clearly tiring from holding the sleeping girl up. He'd been doing it practically all night! "I don't mind, really." In a moment of chivalry, he reached down and lifted Rose's hand to his face, kissing it gently.

No sooner had his lips brushed her hand than Rose sat bolt upright, her eyes wide.

"What's going on?" she asked, looking around. "Did I miss anything?"

The girls all laughed — even Snow joined in — and began to fill Rose in on the evening's events.

"Ella is the Princess of the Ball!" Snow exclaimed.

"And Hagatha and Prunilla got laughed off the stage!" Rapunzel laughed.

"Wow," Rose said. "And I thought it was all a dream!"

"No, it was real," Ella assured her. "Val has been holding you up all night. When he kissed your hand, you . . . woke up."

Rose looked up at Val. "Thanks," she said.

Val blushed. "You're w-welcome," he stammered.

By the time the ball was finally over, it was very late.

"Anyone want a ride home in my carriage?" Rose asked. "There's plenty of room."

"Yes!" the girls chorused.

As they left the ballroom, Madame Taffeta approached Ella.

"I could not help but notice the interesting stitchery on your stepsisters' gowns," she said pointedly. Ella braced herself. She'd been sure she was going to get punished tonight, but not by a teacher!

Madame Taffeta leaned toward Ella slightly. "I can see you do extensive and, shall we say, creative stitching at home," Madame Taffeta went on, her eyes gleaming. "And your stepsisters seem to require careful watching."

Ella nodded, too surprised to say anything. Could it be that a teacher was on her side?

"In light of the situation, I believe it is only fair that you be excused from Stitchery homework for the foreseeable future."

For the second time that night, Ella could not believe her ears. But one look at Madame Taffeta's smiling face told her that her words were true.

"Thank you!" Ella said, giving the teacher a spontaneous hug. Then she hurried to join her friends and tell them the news.

Laughing together, the group traipsed outside to the waiting carriages. The pages were still lined up along the steps and the bridge, but several had fallen asleep.

Val escorted the girls to Rose's carriage, then bowed to them. I will leave you ladies here," he said. "My horse awaits."

The girls scrambled into the carriage. "Bye, Val," Rapunzel called. "See you tomorrow!"

Val waved while the carriage pulled away. Inside, Ella sat back on the lush maroon seat and looked around at her friends. Two weeks ago, she'd felt completely out of place at Princess School. Now she felt right at home. There was no doubt in her mind that with her friends around her, her future at Princess School was as bright as the sparkling tiara that graced the top of her head.

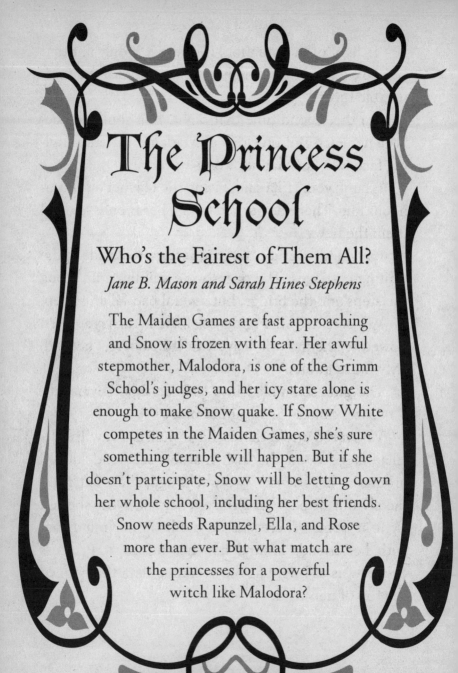

The Princess School

Who's the Fairest of Them All?

Jane B. Mason and Sarah Hines Stephens

The Maiden Games are fast approaching and Snow is frozen with fear. Her awful stepmother, Malodora, is one of the Grimm School's judges, and her icy stare alone is enough to make Snow quake. If Snow White competes in the Maiden Games, she's sure something terrible will happen. But if she doesn't participate, Snow will be letting down her whole school, including her best friends. Snow needs Rapunzel, Ella, and Rose more than ever. But what match are the princesses for a powerful witch like Malodora?

■ SCHOLASTIC